London Dust

Lee Jackson lives in London with his partner Joanne. His first book, *London Dust*, was shortlisted for the Ellis Peters Historical

Also by Lee Jackson

A Metropolitan Murder
The Welfare of the Dead
The Last Pleasure Garden

London Dust

by

Lee Jackson

arrow books

Published by Arrow Books in 2003

7 9 10 8

Arrow Books
The Random House Group Limited
20 Vauxhall Bridge Road, London SW1V 2SA

www.rbooks.co.uk

Addresses for companies within
The Random House Group Limited can be found at:
www.randomhouse.co.uk/offices.htm

The Random House Group Limited Reg. No. 954009

A CIP catalogue record for this book
is available from the British Library

The Random House Group Limited supports The Forest Stewardship Council (FSC), the leading international forest certification organisation. All our titles that are printed on Greenpeace approved FSC certified paper carry the FSC logo. Our paper procurement policy can be found at:
www.rbooks.co.uk/environment

ISBN 9780099439998

Typeset in Bell by MATS, Southend-on-Sea, Essex
Printed and bound in Great Britain by
CPI Antony Rowe, Chippenham, Wiltshire

PART ONE

Chapter One

Blackfriars Bridge

Falling is the easiest method. Just choose the location and take one step forward.

Always be quick about it.

—

I stumble through alleys and courts towards Blackfriars. The fog has swallowed up whole streets, and the wind breathes avalanches of soot into every passage, flecks of ash which trickle from the rooftops like spoiled snow. The shawl which Ellen gave me is all but ruined, the wool peppered with a layer of dust, a powdery mixture of grit and dirt. I pull it tight about my shoulders and hurry onwards, past Saffron Hill, until I come upon a small neglected yard, hidden from the main thoroughfare, where I can pause and catch my breath. The yard itself is nothing more than a huddle of rotting tenements, hunched over a narrow plot of muddy ground. No gas-light has ever shone upon these dwellings, and, in the darkness, each building appears lopsided, shored up at irregular intervals with great struts of timber, leaning in angular contradiction to its neighbour. It is a wretched place, the houses uniform in their dereliction except, perhaps, for the differing degrees of human misery hidden inside. Nothing stirs, however, except the complaint of St. Paul's, echoing against obstinate walls.

One o'clock.

Victoria Street is equally deserted, except for the sound of a distant wagon heading north to King's Cross. I turn the opposite way, to Ludgate, running across the junction, looking out for St Paul's. The upturned bowl of the cathedral is almost invisible, shrouded by dense charcoal clouds that roll down towards the river. The road itself is now lit by gas, a row of flaring jets that stretch down Ludgate Hill to Fleet Street, but, in spite of the lights, it is only when I reach the sloping stretch of road that leads to the bridge that I make out a solitary shabby man, squatting awkwardly on the Portland stone like a mournful gargoyle. He slouches upright as soon as he sees me and blocks my path, extending the traditional upturned palm of a beggar.

'A penny to cross transpontine, Miss . . . or a smacker from your ruby lips?'

He has a face like a cured ham, greasy and fat in equal measure. I look at him sharply, but he merely smiles; he is well aware that respectable women do not travel on foot at such an hour and, besides, how must I look after my long progress through the streets? He watches me closely as I dip into the pocket of my apron and, mercifully, find a penny. He plucks the coin deftly from my hand

and, without another word, bowing ironically, lets me pass. I curse him under my breath.

The fog billows up from the river as I advance across the bridge. After a few yards, I look over my shoulder, and the toll man has all but vanished. I can just make him out, turning his back and shuffling off, his form a shambling silhouette against the halo of Ludgate's muted gaslight. I walk a little further and pause for a minute or so, listening for pedestrians or the clip-clop of a carriage. No-one comes and so I unwrap the shawl and fold it neatly on the pavement. One should always leave something for luck.

I climb up onto the balustrade.

—

'Mr. Shaw, you were on Blackfriars Bridge on the night in question. Tell me, is that correct?'

'Yes, your Lordship.'

'And you spoke to a woman wearing this garment?'

'I believe so, your Honour.'

'Kindly describe the circumstances for us, Mr. Shaw.'

'Well, your Honour, I was resting for a minute or two on that very bridge when a girl steps up wearing that very shawl, what the gentleman is holding, and taps me on the shoulder. She was a brazen young minx, if I may beg your pardon, your Honour, and, to be plain, she was enquiring if I were in want of female affection or, as she put it . . .'

'May I remind you there are ladies present, Mr. Shaw?'

Titters from the gallery.

'My humble apologies, your Honour. Well, if it please your Lordship, I told her to be on her way, on account of my being happily married to a good woman. Now, I believe that must have inflamed her spirits because she just curses me something awful and cuts off. Well, "good riddance" I say to myself, although, to tell the honest truth, I ain't accustomed to hearing such things from a woman. As a matter of fact, I was still recovering my higher faculties when I heard what you would call a splash. Now, that struck me as curious, no two ways about it, and so I turned back and there it was: that self-same garment on the ground, and the girl had gone and vanished. That's the actual facts in plain terms, your Lordship.'

'Can you describe the young woman's features, Mr. Shaw?'

'I could an-a-tomise her, your Honour. She was a very distinctive creature, I'd say, exceedingly tall with very green eyes – reminded me of a cat, in actual fact, your Honour.'

'Your feline acquaintances are of no interest to these proceedings, Mr. Shaw . . .'

Open laughter from the gallery.

'. . . but let us persist in our inquiry in the hope you may enlighten us. Would you consider that the girl's appearance was consistent with the description given by the previous witness, namely the description of Miss Warwick's maidservant?'

'Oh yes, I'd say so, Sir.'

It takes a certain strength of will to throw yourself off.

Practise losing your balance, if that helps.

I perch on the edge for a moment, trying to catch a final glimpse of St. Paul's through the fog. Nothing comes of that, so I lean forward and, like a practised diver, bend and fall headlong. There is no need to jump. Much better to drop like ripe fruit.

The stone supports fly past my face, and, for a moment, I have the distinct sensation of floating upwards. Then the river slaps me sideways and draws me in, spinning like a top, skirts tearing, catching on some unseen jetsam, petticoats billowing in the current.

I cross my fingers and pray for forgiveness.

Chapter Two

Bow Street to Holywell Street

Henry Shaw waits at the rear of the court to hear the coroner's verdict upon the death of Ellen Warwick.

'Wilful Murder by Person or Persons Unknown.'

He cannot hear the rest, since a dozen newspaper men snatch up their pages of shorthand and depart noisily from the room, vying with each other to be first to report this conclusion to their public. Shaw tries to catch their attention, hoping for an opportunity to recount his story once more, but each man escapes him. In consequence, as the beadle draws proceedings to a close, he makes his way through the gossiping crowd alone and quite unnoticed. He is satisfied, at least, by his performance as a witness and relishes the novelty of departing the building without the assistance of Her Majesty's Police. Indeed, he cannot help but smile as he stands on the court steps and surveys the traffic racing along Bow Street. As he dons his hat, however, he notices a familiar face: a boy leaning against the nearby railings with hands shoved in his pockets. The youth, a wiry lad of thirteen years or thereabouts with matted black hair and dressed in dirty corduroys, nods and ambles towards him.

'The beak let you off again, Harry?'

'Mis-ter Shaw to you,' he says playfully, pronouncing each syllable in mock indignation. 'Or you may call me "Papa", should anyone be enquiring. And, dear boy, as you well know, I was merely assisting the administration of justice.'

'My Pa's in Newgate, Mis-ter Shaw, or that's what Ma says, anyways.'

'That's as may be, young Master Tip, but I don't reckon he would raise objections to the appropriation of his paternal monicker in the course of our business.'

The boy shrugs and follows Shaw as he sets off towards the Strand.

'And why am I blest with your particular attention today, Master Tip?'

'Message from Ma.'

Shaw stops beside the colonnade of the Royal Lyceum and grabs the boy tightly by his arm. 'And how long should we wait for this blessed bulletin?'

The boy shrugs once more, apparently oblivious to his grip. Shaw releases him and sighs in mock exasperation. 'In your own time.'

'Ma said to tell you that she tried that gent from the *Weekly Argus*, but he ain't keen, on account of the manservant Quill what already talked.'

'Is that it?' asks Shaw.

'No. She said "Have a word with Bowles". She said you'd know what she meant.'

Shaw curls his lip, 'Old Bowles? He still at it? I thought he was dead. Well, I suppose we could do worse. What's the phrase?'

'Beggars can't be choosers, Mis-ter Shaw?'

'Quite. Well, we must not ignore your good mother's advice, must we? Follow me,' he says, immediately striding off in the direction of the river. 'Come on, keep up.'

The boy follows as Shaw tries to set a fast pace. They soon find, however, that every street surrounding Covent Garden is congested with traffic intent on departing the market, the daily exodus of barrows, donkey-carts and waggons that trundle in slow procession to the Strand, and thence homewards. It is some time, therefore, before they finally make their way down Wellington Street and through the crowds to St. Mary's Church. From there, fortunately, it is a short distance to the confines of Holywell Street; it is an older, narrower thoroughfare than those surrounding it, and the houses, a gabled relic of the time of Elizabeth, are home to printshops and booksellers of low repute. Half-way along, they come upon their destination, a run-down little shop, which, contrary to all its neighbours, does not even boast a single counter of books upon the pavement. There is nothing, in fact, to give the impression that it may be open for business.

J. F. Bowles
Purveyor of Cartographical Antiquities
Holywell Street, Strand.

Paint peels from the sign in curling black strips, and the window is thick with grime. On a whim, Shaw rubs away a little of the dirt upon the glass and peers inside at the display: a dozen antique leather volumes entitled *Tabulae Orbis Terrarum*, each one meticulously laid out on green baize, their spines flaking dried glue and gold leaf. The boy, meanwhile, rattles the door handle and finds it open. He goes inside, forcing Shaw to follow in his footsteps. The interior of the shop, no more than ten feet square all told, is filled with piles of books and bindings, to the exclusion of all else. Some of the larger works have been heaped horizontally into makeshift columns, the supports for several scaffolds of wooden shelves, rising like literary pyramids, with accumulations of small crown octavos at their summit. Indeed, these edifices almost entirely obscure an elderly man, sitting on a high stool in the centre of the room, dressed in the frock coat and knee breeches of an earlier generation. He appears to work in near darkness, for the only light that falls upon him is the meagre glimmer which filters through the glass of the shop window. This is sufficient, however, to illuminate the flurry of dust that heralds Shaw and Tip's arrival as they open the door, prompting the old man to look up from his labours and peer beyond his visitors, as if counting every mote which has escaped into the street and planning a method of recapture.

'Can I assist you, gentlemen?' he mutters.

'Well,' says Shaw, 'it's more a case of being the furtherance of your own interests, Sir. You see . . .'

The old man ignores him and clambers clumsily off his chair onto a footstool composed of the later volumes of McGarry's *Infant Encyclopedia.* He leans towards a shelf and pulls out a slim volume, beckoning the boy over to his side.

'Do you like maps, my boy? Or perhaps pictures, hmm?'

'Don't know,' replies the boy, surprised by the question.

'Ah, but there are all types of map, you see?' he says, opening the book. 'Have a look at this print, young master, eh? It's a lithographic likeness of Verioni's "Ancipites Corpora", hmm? Do you know it? Can you see how he's filled out the *contours* of their skin? That brings the countryside to life, eh?'

The old man coughs with pleasure as the boy's eyes widen.

'That's disgusting,' exclaims Tip, avidly flicking over the pages.

The old man chuckles. 'No, my dear boy, a lesson for you. If you are within these premises, you call it *artistic.*'

Shaw suppresses a rueful smile as he leans over to catch a glimpse of the lithographs of naked bodies. 'I didn't know that was in your line, Mr. Bowles, the pleasures of the flesh? I took you for a scholar.'

'And, indeed I am, Mr. . . .' the old man looks at him peevishly.

'Shaw, Henry Shaw.'

'Indeed, I am, Mr. Shaw, but the young should be prepared for all our social evils, don't you think? Ignorance is a terrible thing, is it not?'

'I'd guess this one here is better prepared than most, but he'll please himself. If you please, Sir, I'm here about Ellen Warwick ...'

The old man stares at him blankly.

'The singer that was murdered?' continues Shaw. 'You've heard the story I presume? I have some particular information about the circumstances . . .'

The old man tuts, interrupting Shaw again. 'I've no interest in murders, Mr. Tom, Dick or Harry or whoever you are, no interest at all.'

Shaw raises his eyes heavenwards. 'If you let me finish it, Sir, you'll find I'm getting to Miss Warwick's servant girl, the one they reckon killed her. *I* was the last one what saw her before she jumped in the river. In fact,' he says, leaning towards the old man and lowering his voice to a confidential whisper, 'I've just come from the inquest this very moment.'

The old man's face brightens, and he clutches Shaw's hand solicitously, leading him to the stool.

'A suicide? Why did you not say? Sit down, Mr. Shaw. Please have a seat. Tell me everything you know, hmm? What was her name, this child?'

'Natalie Meadows, so they tell me, Sir,' replies Shaw, evidently pleased to have caught his attention, 'but let me put it to you from the start, if you will . . .'

Shaw seats himself upon the vacant seat. Whilst Tip browses the shelves, he begins to relate the incident to the old man, embellishing upon his conversation with the girl on the bridge and adding a wealth of spurious detail. In fact, he replies at convincing length to several questions concerning the girl's appearance and demeanour, and, although it takes him a good ten minutes or more to finish his account, the old man appears thoroughly gratified. More significantly, as he had hoped, Bowles finally gives Shaw two shillings for his trouble. Once this peculiar transaction is concluded, the man and boy depart the premises.

'Queer business that,' comments the boy, scowling, as they turn back down Holywell Street.

'An old fool,' says Shaw, weighing the coins in his hand, 'but a most profitable business for us, and so we ask no further questions. What say we treat ourselves on the proceeds?'

The boy agrees and Shaw smiles. His eye lights upon the boy's jacket. 'What's that I see in your pocket? Can it be that you have been a tad light-fingered?' He purses his lips in impression of a disgruntled school-mistress, observing the very book which Bowles showed them earlier.

'Just some reading matter', says the boy, stuffing it deeper inside his pocket, 'to further complete my education.'

Shaw smiles. 'Don't tell your mother.'

—

Bowles waits until the man and boy have left the shop, then locks the door behind them. He turns to one of the more cluttered shelves and retrieves a thick ledger, taking it back to his stool. His eyesight is failing him, and he squints as he props it upon his knee and completes a new entry in ornate script:

Name:	*Natalie Meadows*
Death:	*Self-murder, drowning*
Situation:	*Blackfriars Bridge, East*
Character:	*Young female, servant. Suspicion in mistress's death*
Notes:	*Informant an opportunist, perhaps a liar? Discarded shawl – meaning?*

When he has finished, he turns to the last page and unfolds a creased parchment, faithfully glued against the spine. He leans on the body of the book and brings the yellowing vellum close to his nose as he scratches it with his pen, making some brief calculations before tracing an arc from Ludgate to Wapping, marking a cross upon the banks of the river.

Chapter Three

Wapping

Daylight. I am breathing again, retching but breathing, my body sunk in the mess of the river, washed ashore at low tide. Either side of me are a series of rickety wharves, apparently fallen into disuse, their timbers poking into the water like crippled fingers. On the bank, meanwhile, sit warehouses, all boarded up and closed.

I cannot move for the mud.

The river always gives up its dead.

Who told me that? It is true.

I wake up to the sensation of coarse hands tugging at my shoulders, nails scraping my skin. Instinctively, I flail out but only to be dropped back into the mire, and the mud sucks me back down readily enough. I can just raise my head high enough to see a stocky man standing a few feet away, dressed in dirty oilskins. He walks in front of me up to the nearest warehouse and sits down upon the steps, watching me all the while. His face suggests he is forty years of age or more; he is a little old for a mud-lark, but undoubtedly some kind of river scavenger, no doubt the owner of a small skiff which I can just make out, moored beside one of the wharves. He continues watching me in silence for what seems like several minutes, and I cannot summon the strength to do anything about it. Then he speaks in a deliberate drawl.

'I took you for dead, Missy.'

'I'm not.'

'That's plain enough,' he says. 'Been swimming?'

'I don't know if that's any of your business,' I reply hoarsely, still barely able to move.

He stares at me but says nothing.

'Look,' I continue, 'you can see I have nothing of value . . .'

He looks genuinely aggrieved. 'It's none of my business if you go drowning with the high tide neither, Missy. However, it's plain you're doing pretty fine at taking care of yourself, on account of which we find you washed up here like so much driftwood, so I wishes you good luck.'

He gets up and clambers up the steps and onto the wharf. He is quite right. I do need his help.

'Wait, I'm sorry,' I shout after him, 'I didn't mean any harm. Perhaps if you could just help me up? I can hardly move my legs.'

He stops and turns slowly, as if pondering the consequences, then jumps back down to the beach, swinging an arm around my waist and lunging me upright with unexpected force. I can barely stand unsupported and lean against his side as I pull up the remains of my skirts to examine my legs. Although the sensation begins to trickle back into the bruised flesh, I still have to grab hold of his arm to steady myself. He looks at me with pity. Or perhaps it is contempt.

'I think you'd better be coming with me, Missy, unless you have other plans?'

Again, I am too weak to argue. I nod my agreement.

The walking is agony, but he leads me patiently from the shore, up the warehouse steps and onto the quay. Finally, he picks me up bodily and lowers me into the skiff. The boat is empty but for some hessian sacking, which I pull round my chest for warmth, watching as he nimbly climbs in, takes up the oars and heaves with the current.

He maintains his silence as we travel upstream, and I begin to recognise the leisurely curve of the river by Wapping Basin. After a few minutes, he pulls towards a small jetty on the south side of the water, a landing which lies opposite the ships waiting to enter St. Katherine's Docks. On the shore, an old woman and a gaggle of children line the bank, scraping the mud with wooden planks, sifting it for discarded sea-coal or other riches. A couple of them stop and stare as he moors the boat, until the woman chides them back to work. My benefactor, meanwhile, drags me out of the boat towards the dilapidated shacks that crest the bank, the timber shanties of those who make a meagre living from the river. When we come to a particular doorway, fashioned from rotten wood that appears to have been reclaimed from some sunken vessel, he takes me inside. The room, if such a word can be used, is tiny and spartan, even for a solitary man: on one side, there is a wooden pallet bedded with straw; on the opposite side, there is a black kettle, matchbox and a poor man's hearth, improvised from tiles and broken bricks. Nothing more. He lays me upon the bed, then walks over to this fireplace and lights a match, solemnly mixing up splintered fragments of driftwood and coal until an acrid smoke rises in black gusts, barely escaping through the small flue hewn in the ceiling. I am grateful for the heat, nonetheless.

'You need dry clothes and some food in your belly,' he says bluntly.

'Yes, I believe I do.'

'Will you wait here and give no trouble?' he says.

I nod, coughing, and he walks towards the doorway. He turns his head and says, 'And will you give me your name, Missy?'

'I don't know yours.'

'Thomas Cave. There's no need for games, Missy, it won't do no harm to tell me your name.'

'Flora.'

He ponders this for a moment then leaves. I am not sure if he believed me.

~

Natalie Meadows is dead.

That is the thing to remember now.

~

It is a good hour or so before he returns, though I am ill equipped to judge the passing of time. I listen to the tide lapping at the shore, until I can hear the strokes of the oars on the water and the creaking of the jetty as he ties up the boat. It is a minute or two more until the door swings ajar and he backs into the room, dragging an open packing crate behind him. There is a brown paper parcel on top, wrapped roughly with string, which he takes and places to one side. As for the crate itself, he pulls it up beside the bed, and, as I look inside, I cannot help but gasp in amazement. It is filled with female clothing: dresses and jackets, bonnets, boots, hats and gloves, all pressed neatly down under the cage of an expansive hoop petticoat. None of it is quite in the latest fashion, but it is a proper lady's wardrobe all the same, all folded and packed away. There is even a small hand-mirror stashed to one side. Cave resolutely ignores my surprise and opens out the first parcel on the floor to reveal a quartern loaf and a quarterpound of cheese.

'Get out of those damn rags afore you catch your death,' he says, 'then we can eat.'

For a moment, I wonder whether he is more anxious to eat or see me naked, but, before I can respond, he wanders unbidden back outside; I assume it is the former. What can I do but root through the box? It is all quality. If my body were not half-frozen, I might try everything on. As it is, I strip out of my rags as quick as I can, using them to wipe off as much of the dirt as possible. I slip on a pair of longcloth drawers, pulling them over my benumbed dirty legs, though it seems a crime to spoil such pristine fabric. Then comes the crinoline and a silk chemise; I flick through the gowns until I uncover something that may be suitable, an embroidered day dress in Azoff poplin. It takes some time struggling with the unfamiliar stays, but, once I am done, it all fits quite well. There is even a matching mantle, a heavy fabric beaded with intricate Ottoman designs and a winter bonnet to top it off. In truth, I cannot remember if I ever wore anything quite so precious.

I recall the mirror. I bend down and dare to gaze at my reflection: a young woman dressed in green, thin with bedraggled russet hair and large hazel eyes, twenty-three years at most. Almost pretty, if I say so myself, if it were not for some bruising about the face and the dregs of the river in my hair. I must pray no-one looks too closely.

The door opens ajar, and, from the other side, Cave says, 'Done?'

I smile at this gallantry and beckon him in.

'Where did you get this?'

'Well,' he says, 'let's just say I have a few pals on the packet steamers with butter-fingers, and let's leave it at that.'

'And they just happened to catch this particular box before it was ruined?'

'If it troubles you, Missy, just think of it as salvage.'

'You realise I cannot repay you?'

'I'll seek my rewards in the hereafter, as I'm not accustomed to finding them down here, don't you worry.' He smiles but then his face soon turns serious once more. 'Now, tell us, what were you playing at, ending up half-drowned?'

'An accident. I was lucky you found me – I should thank you.'

'Luck ain't the word and thanks not required,' he says, looking at me sceptically, 'and you don't have to tell, if you don't want. Come then, let's eat.'

He bends over the parcel of food and tears me a piece of bread and a chunk of cheese. I watch as he devours his share, catching the breadcrumbs in his cupped hand and licking his fingers clean. My own stomach aches for food, and so I follow his example. It is only when it is all gone that he bites his lip in concentration and looks up at me. 'So, Missy, where are you bound? I ain't got no room here, you see that.'

'No,' I reply, 'I've a sister in Bethnal Green. I'll see if she'll have me for a while.'

I might as well have a sister in Buckingham Palace.

He looks thoughtful and nods. 'Very good, Missy, now you're thinking it through. We'll set you on an even keel yet. I can take you back across the water before nightfall, if you like.'

'I've a friend in Wapping – she might lend me a couple of pennies for lodging. Can you take me there?'

—

Another lie, but it will do.

Wapping is as good as anywhere.

—

At my request, Cave takes me to the nearest pump where I can, at least, clean my face and hair. We pass by a few women who stare at me, doubtless wondering how I came by such an outfit, but nothing is said; they seem to know Cave and keep their distance. The water proves to be the usual brown muck, dredged up from Lord knows where, and I wonder if it is an improvement. I cannot hope for anything better. When I am finished, he leads me directly to the boat, and, once we are on board, he rows quickly across the river, his back turned towards the opposite shore and the dismal battlements of the Tower. We soon reach a landing place, just east of St. Katherine's Docks and I bid him goodbye, unsure what to say beyond thanking him once more. He is a peculiar man, and he seems to expect nothing more of me. He merely nods, exchanges a couple of words with the nearby lightermen and strikes back for the south bank.

I make my way up the quayside steps to Wapping High Street. I am used to going about unnoticed, and I should know better. The dress garners attention as soon as I emerge onto the road, even though it is almost dark and no-one can contrast its finery with my dirty face; warehouse men shout practised catcalls; screaming gangs of children take me for a charity woman and perform cartwheels in front of me, tugging at my skirts. I do my best to ignore them, bowing my head and quickening my pace, even though I have no real destination in mind. A few hundred yards further on, past the Black Boy Tavern, I realise that I have come as far as the station-house of the Marine Police. There is a noticeboard by the gas-light, which projects from the building, with a weathered piece of paper torn from a penny rag and, no doubt, pinned up by some literate wag:

Miss Warwick's Tragic Death

It is some months since Miss Ellen Warwick last graced the London stage as 'The Brick Lane Butterfly', but this has not lessened the sensation generated by the brutal manner of her death. Inspector Burton has taken considerable pains to inform the fair sex, in the light of this tragedy, of appropriate measures which they may undertake to ensure their safety. We welcome this sage counsel but trust the Inspector is not employed merely in an advisory capacity . . .

The rest is missing, but I can guess how it ends.

Chapter Four

Shepherdess Walk

'Last graced the stage'?

They were never quite so fond of her when she was alive. Still, I recall it perfectly.

Ellen's final engagement was at the Eagle, not long after Arthur Wilkes became proprietor. It was a warm July evening, a Saturday; the gardens were glorious in full bloom, and the famous rotunda had just been decked out in new gilding, lit by glimmering gas-lights installed between the Grecian columns. Her billing, *'Positively the Final Appearance Before an Appreciative Public'*, had doubled the audience for that evening, and, by the time I reached the stalls, I found that the benches were packed quite full. I squeezed myself next to a young woman nursing a babe underneath a tatty red shawl. She smiled at me whilst cradling the child.

'Come to see off the Butterfly, dear?'

I said that I had. I peeled the orange I had bought from one of the hawkers. I must have seen

Ellen fifty times before. Probably we both had. She was, in her way, quite famous.

O Butterfly, O Butterfly,
Come flitting o'er the lea,
You would not want to fly so high
if you had care for me.

Ellen detested that song.

The organ started up with 'I Gazed Upon The Blessed Dawn'. The Chairman rose and began by introducing a comic mime, a new act whose cavorting hardly raised a murmur in the crowd. Most of the audience ignored him and turned instead to its supper, unwrapping fried sole or the Eagle's patent ham sandwiches as the house's waiters began to move between the rows, carrying precariously balanced trays of porter and bottled stout. Whoops of ironical delight bellowed up from the stalls as the mime finally abandoned the stage and was replaced by a bickering pair of 'gentleman costermongers'. This was more acceptable and shouts of 'Go to it', 'Give it him' and the like rang through the hall as they swapped mock blows; after them, a young operatic female, very much in the manner of a low Jenny Lind with sundry nods and winks; then, a quintet of Italian tumblers, amusing only due to their incompetence. There were others: the Incomparable Emmeline and her Celebrated Impostures, a dire impersonator of forgotten thespians; Carlo the Quizzical Clown, Italian by trade, rather than ancestry, the Jolly Jenkins singing 'Please Don't Sell Drink to Father': quite affecting and comical. I had a fondness for Jenkins, but I remember them all.

Finally, at ten o'clock or thereabouts, the menagerie played the refrain of 'Butterfly', and Ellen emerged from the wings. She was wearing an evening dress of pink satin trimmed with lace and looked quite beautiful. Hush descended on the audience as she removed the pins from her hair, letting blonde locks tumble down over her shoulders. She smiled her faint smile, whispered a modest 'good evening', and launched into 'The Dandy Husband', an old favourite from the penny gaffs, a song that she sang before she was so well-known. The crowd attended to her voice as if it were salvation itself, hanging upon every line, mumbling the words as she sang them. She ran through her usual repertoire, the applause growing more vigorous with each piece, and she finished an hour or so later with 'Butterfly', accepting only one encore, as was her habit. And then came a thunder of applause, stamping of feet, whistles and calls for more. But there was no more.

The lights were lit, and the crowd dispersed, leaving the usual detritus of broken bottles and orange peel, congratulating each other on being the last individuals in London to have heard Ellen Warwick sing.

This was not strictly true, of course, as she often sang for me.

The dressing room at the Eagle was cold and damp, having been used as an outhouse for the gardens in an earlier incarnation. Nevertheless, it was indicative of her status that Ellen had any such private space at all. When I entered, she was struggling with her costume behind a painted silk screen, gracefully illuminated by a row of spluttering candles. Across the room sat Jemima, a voluminous old woman of ruddy complexion, dressed in faded cream with a ribboned cap atop her rosy forehead, huffing to herself like a dormant volcano. Her companion, a miniature French poodle, rested in her lap, snoring in the seemingly endless folds of her skirts. Jemima had been employed at the Eagle since time immemorial, although no-one could tell you in precisely what capacity. Ellen saw me and grinned, putting on her usual patter.

'Nat! Ain't this jolly! I didn't know you was coming.'

'Very comical, Ellie.' She knew I followed her from place to place like a moonstruck baby.

'So, dear,' she said, slipping out from behind the screen, dressed now in plain white muslin, 'do you think they liked it?'

She was joking, of course; Ellen was never one to doubt herself.

'I think so,' I replied, smiling.

Ellen nodded, absent-mindedly, at my reply. She had already sat down and begun pencilling a fresh page to what she called her 'account book', a little black diary which she kept religiously; she had a good head for figures, and it was something of a ritual to tally her income after every performance.

'We likes her, don't we, Spoonikins?' the old woman abruptly exclaimed, addressing herself to the somnolent lapdog. 'We likes Miss Nelly but we doesn't like that other one, do we, Spooney? Not her.'

She was pointing at me. Ellen was surprised at this and looked up from her book-keeping. 'Jemmy, what do you mean?'

'Means what I says, that's all. She ain't no good, Nelly.' The old harridan turned to me, quoting off by heart, '"Natalie Meadows, there she stands, Queen of the Grecian *Pose Plastique*, Positively Guaranteed to Astound." Ha!' Then she went back to stroking the poodle, as suddenly as she had begun.

'Don't heed her, dear,' said Ellen, whispering to me. 'She ain't been right since her old man went and left her.'

I shrugged. It was odd that she remembered my own meagre theatrical debut, but the old woman, however, was already half asleep, muttering something to herself. 'Anyhow, Ellie,' I changed tack, 'I hear you're still settled on calling it a day?'

'Wonderfully settled, as it happens. In fact, I might be able to help *you* out, if you're still in queer street, that is.'

'How's that?'

'I'm opening up a regular little business, Nat, all above board . . .'

I tutted. 'I don't know why you don't stick with it, Ellie; they all adore you. Charlie Morton said he'd give you a regular spot at the Canterbury, and you know he would.'

Ellen shook her head, 'Nat, it's hardly the bleedin' Theatre Royal. Anyhow, I'm thirty, sweets, and I ain't getting any younger, and I want to do something more respectable. You know how it is.'

'Well, what will it be, this business?'

'Ellen Warwick's Family Mourning Establishment.'

I must have laughed, because she looked daggers at me.

'It's bought and paid for, Nat. You'd be perfect behind the counters, on account of being so ladylike.'

She meant on account of being so tall, but I let that pass. 'And who paid for it?' I asked. She ignored my question.

'Think about it. I'll need someone. You'd be good company.'

I said nothing, and let her finish writing up her accounts.

—

Jemmy was still sleeping when we snuffed out the candles, and we knew better than trying to wake her. We made our way through the gas-lit gardens out to the main gates where Arthur Wilkes, the proprietor, slumped over the ticket stand, apparently counting the night's takings. He was a stooped little man with narrow eyes and pinched lips and hadn't owned the place for many months. Everyone called him 'The Weasel', though never to his face.

'Goodnight, ladies. And may I hazard to say, Nelly, that it's a crying shame, and you knows it? Are you sure you won't be reconsidering leaving us?'

Ellen smiled a thin smile, 'Not for a minute, Arthur.'

'Well,' said the Weasel, sliding neatly between us and clamping an arm around Ellen's waist, 'you know you'll always have a fine welcome at the Eagle, uncommon fine.'

Ellen gently removed his roving fingers and said, 'You're a jolly old party, Arthur, and I'll be sure to remember the kind offer. Now, pay up and we'll part company, fair and square.'

The Weasel shrugged and dropped a small pouch of coins into Ellen's hand. 'You'll be always welcome, Nelly, and don't forget it.'

She smiled and bid him goodbye. We walked on, and, as we turned into the City Road, Ellen clapped her hands on the pouch and said. 'That's that. Now come on, sweets, please won't you help us out? You've got the look for mourning.'

'Thank you,' I said, pulling a face. 'There's a fine compliment.'

'I speak as I find,' she replied.

I was about to argue the point when a boy came running up to us, appearing from the shadows of a nearby doorway. He was no more than eleven or twelve years of age; a little lean-faced street arab with a tangle of thick black hair.

'Miss . . . Miss Warwick . . .'

'Well?' she asked quizzically, more amused than

annoyed, accustomed to such attention. 'There ain't no money returned, you know.'

'It's not that ... it's ... it's ...' the boy stammered, 'well, I heard you ain't singing no more after tonight ...'

'That's right,' she replied.

'Well ...' said the boy, blushing, 'it's ... it ain't right.'

She laughed and thanked him very grandly for his concern. The boy, meanwhile, simply stood there, apparently having exhausted his sentiments. Ellen looked down at him and, after a moment's hesitation, delved into her purse, retrieving a small piece of card. 'And this is for you, for being so kind.'

The boy tentatively took the card and squinted at it. I could see it was a miniature portrait of Ellen herself, a photograph showing her posing in her finest black satin gown. He looked up at her in wonderment.

'Go on then,' she said. 'It's for keeping.'

The boy grinned and, clutching it to his chest, took one last glance at her and ran off down the City Road.

'That did the trick, didn't it?' she said, recovering an identical card from her purse. 'Well, what do you reckon? It's a *carte de visite*. I had them made up for the shop.'

Her picture was on one side, her name and the address of the new business were printed upon the other.

'It's a good likeness,' I replied. 'Can I have one?'

'Lor'!' she exclaimed, laughing. 'Don't you see enough of me?'

Chapter Five

New Oxford Street

Henry Shaw Esquire and his youthful companion, having spent the money they acquired from Mr. Bowles upon a substantial luncheon of eel pie, stand in joint admiration of the wares displayed in the window of James Smith & Sons (Sticks and Umbrellas) Ltd. Rack upon rack of sticks and gamps now lie before them in the window, some plain, some ornate. An astute observer might notice a glazed expression upon their faces: a peculiar concentration upon the street as reflected in the glass. Tip fiddles restlessly with the buttons on his jacket.

'Is the dray still there, my boy?'

'Looks like it, don't it?'

'Then, let us prolong our perusal of these parapluvial appliances until it ain't,' Shaw snaps, 'and you remember to call me "Pa" or we'll go back and tell your blessed mother we haven't turned tuppence. And don't play with that blasted jacket.'

The boy looks up at him sullenly and goes back to contemplating the umbrellas. Finally, he speaks again.

'Dray's gone. Traffic's moving.'

'Very well, my dear boy,' says Shaw, turning to face a stall on the opposite side of the street and raising his voice. 'Do go and purchase a copy of the *Daily News* for your Papa, there's a good lad.'

Shaw presents a penny to him with a theatrical flourish. Tip, in turn, snatches it from his outstretched hand, dodging as Shaw attempts to pat him on the head, and discreetly surveys the street. Then, resigned to his fate, he dashes headlong into the traffic, darting with expert carelessness into the path of a barouche. Although they are travelling at no more than a steady trot, the horses rear up in surprise and almost unseat their driver. The boy, meanwhile, slumps into the dirt a few feet in front of them with an almost acrobatic precision that would enrapture the most accomplished tumbler. Immediately, a piercing cry reverberates down the street, albeit somewhat prematurely.

'Dead!'

Shaw dashes over to the youth's side and cradles his preternaturally limp body in his arms.

'Dead! My darling boy killed!'

The distraught driver, a corpulent young man, bounces down beside them, his ample jowls twitching in shock. Meanwhile, as if summoned by an invisible bailiff, a semi-circle of onlookers gathers to watch the drama unfold. The older members of the crowd talk in low whispers and a line of clerks and office boys shoulder themselves into the foreground. No-one does anything.

Tip, obligingly, coughs and opens one eye.

Murmurs of 'Praise God' and 'Thank the Lord' bubble through the assembled crowd.

'Pa . . . is . . . is that you?' he says, gazing up listlessly into the clouded sky.

'Yes, my boy, here . . . here I am,' stutters Shaw, tears pouring down his ruddy cheeks.

'Pa – it's so dark,' he wheezes, 'Pa, so very dark.'

Murmurs of 'Blinded, poor thing!' and 'He can't see!' A couple of the shop boys begin to lay odds against his recovery.

As the crowd grows, an elderly gentleman emerges from the carriage, supported by a pale young woman. He is blessed with aquiline features and dressed entirely in clerical black; the girl, meanwhile, wears a white morning dress and bonnet. As a result, they resemble two misplaced chess pieces. He stands and watches the scene, taking stock, then addresses himself to the trembling driver.

'Albert, what is the meaning of this?'

The large young man blanches and wobbles, a mute testament to his undoubted guilt.

Murmurs of 'Shame!' and 'He 'alf killed 'im!' from the crowd.

The old clergyman, however, pays no further heed to his employee and shakes his head solemnly, turning to Shaw.

'My poor man, this is a terrible calamity, most terrible. Let us convey the child to a physician . . .'

'Well,' Shaw interrupts, 'a thousand thanks, Your Reverence, but I thinks his father can take care of him best . . . we ain't so blessed with the pecuniary necessities, of course, but he might be well cared for at home, if his mother were not so poorly herself . . .'

Tip rises up upon his elbows, then sinks back into Shaw's arms.

'Of course, of course. Self-reliance!' intones the clergyman. 'Admirable, very admirable, a Christian virtue!'

Shaw's face sags – this was not the effect he intended. However, the clergyman continues.

'Nevertheless, I would be failing in my Christian duty were I to allow you to proceed on this course without some token of practical assistance. One moment, if you please.'

He clambers back into the carriage, aided again by the silent young woman. After what seems an age, he returns and slips a folded note into a dog-eared envelope, which he hands to Shaw.

'Take this, my dear man. It may provide some comfort, and God speed.'

Murmurs of 'Very proper' and 'There's quality' from the crowd.

'Thank you, your Reverence, thank you. We'll do our best for the little fellow, poor chap,' says Shaw, taking the envelope and tucking it in his breast pocket, then drawing Tip's body up onto the pavement.

'Indeed, I am sure of it!' he says, patting Shaw on the shoulder and leading the young woman back into the barouche. 'Onwards, Albert.'

Young Albert calms the horses and, scowling, ascends to his seat, driving the carriage off down the crowded street, accompanied by ripe language from a queue of traffic that trails back as far as St.

Giles Circus. Shaw and Tip, on the other hand, struggle to their feet and limp pathetically in the opposite direction, humbly accepting a couple of pennies from the dispersing crowd as they do so. When they are satisfied that no-one has followed them, they stop beside the church of St. Giles and rest on a flat gravestone in the churchyard. The boy shakes off his injuries with the muck from his clothes, but Shaw ignores his companion and reaches inside his jacket. He retrieves the clergyman's gift, opening the envelope and turning it inside-out, looking for a bank note. Instead, a piece of folded print falls loose with a title that reads:

The Society for the Propoundment of Hygienic Christianity
A Guide to the Necessary Ablutions for Christian Cleanliness
Recounted in Good Faith by the Reverend Hengist Wallace
Not for Sale

'Blow me,' exclaims Shaw.

The boy smiles. 'Ma's goin' to kill you, Harry.'

Chapter Six

Little White Lion Street

The last fugitive rays of daylight slope into the vicinity of Seven Dials, disappearing into dingy attic rooms. Shops begin to close their shutters and retire for the night. Women draw in the neighbourly canopy of laundry strung between houses, spraying impromptu showers onto the street below. Some grab their dirty children and sling them indoors. Others merely linger in doorways, and, on every corner, barracking men loiter in the gin-shops. Everything sinks into darkness as the evening tide of cheap humanity ebbs and flows around Shaw and Tip. They notice none of it. Shaw sighs and speaks to the boy.

'Master Tip, what say we forget this afternoon's unfortunate circumstances and not give trouble to your dear Ma?'

The boy looks thoughtful then says, 'What's left?'

'Ninepence all told.'

The boy looks up at him.

'Well, give it us, Harry, and Ma won't hear a word from me.'

Shaw pauses in his step, frowning. Grudgingly, he slips a hand into his trouser pocket and pulls out the change.

'Maybe I've managed to teach you something after all, my boy.'

The boy snatches the money from Shaw's hand. 'Maybe you have.'

They cross the Dials junction and head down Little White Lion Street. The Little White Lion public house stands upon the corner of a row of little shops, propped up on one side by Bilcher's Urban Comestibles, a more solid construction seemingly designed to support its drunken neighbour. Tip pushes open the door of the Lion and runs inside, and, once more, Shaw follows behind him. The interior is narrow and smoky, a single room lit by brass oil lamps, each dangling precariously from the low rafters. The hearth offers up muted warmth and a trio of glum men sits about it, slouching on rickety wooden chairs, puffing on their pipes. Nearer to the bar, inhabitants of the Dials, the admirable Bilcher included, crouch on low seats around a deal table, intent upon a succession of playing cards and pennies which circulate around the table, but none of which seem to move quite to their mutual satisfaction. The only other furniture in the room is the bar itself, a long mahogany altar, its chipped surface supplying the requisite support for patrons in various stages of mental disarray. Behind this venerable feature sit twin shelves of assorted bottles, a selection of cordials and liquors, many of them coated with dust, and a small woman, aged forty or so, perched on a high stool. She applies a greasy cloth to two tumblers, peering intently at the offending articles, whilst a pair of young men, copy-clerks who pride themselves on being rather smart for the Lion, lean against the bar in front of her, juggling a slurred conversation and, when inspiration fails them, draw upon her opinion. She looks up and beams her most radiant smile at Tip's arrival.

'Hallo, Ma,' says Tip, winking.

'My little angel!' she exclaims, leaning forward to kiss his forehead.

'Hallo, Milly,' says Shaw, removing his hat and sitting at the bar. 'I'll have a drop of Bass pale, thanks for asking.'

'I thinks, *Sir*,' interrupts one of the clerks, laying unnecessary stress on that syllable and swinging his head in Shaw's direction, 'that the *lady* were serving my colleague here.'

'Yes, don't be so rude, Harry,' says Tip's mother, pouring the liquor from a musty brandy bottle into the young man's glass, 'and, besides, what have you been doing to my boy? He looks knocked about.'

'I ain't been knocked about by him,' protests the boy.

'Not knocked about, my dear Milly,' says Shaw, talking over the boy's protestations, 'just the roseate glow as is natural from a long day's toil. Really, there ain't no need to mollycoddle him so.'

'Is this person distressing you, Missus?' says the second young man, waving a finger at Shaw, levering himself from the bar into an uneasy compromise with gravity.

'No need for concern, thanking you, Sir,' says Tip's mother to the clerk, hastily pouring him another dollop of brandy, 'Mr. Shaw here is, as you might say, employed in an educative capacity respecting my dear boy.'

'I ain't been knocked about by him,' says the boy again, emphatically.

'We believe,' continues his mother, 'that my Tip has talents what might be drawn out with proper education.'

'An education is wonderful advantageous,' agrees the first clerk, nodding sagely and looking at Shaw, 'though depending on the teacher.'

'It was the bleeding horse what done it – not him!' says Tip forcefully, staring at his feet as he speaks.

'Shut your trap,' murmurs Shaw.

'Horse!' exclaims Milly, 'a horse?'

'My kingdom for a horse!' exclaims the second clerk, inordinately delighted with himself.

Shaw smiles weakly and says, 'It's what he's good at, Milly. We've got to nurture his talents, like what we agreed.'

'I won't stand for that sort of caper, Harry,' she replies sharply, going back to rubbing furiously away at a mottled glass, then dabbing her eyes with the rag. 'My boy, my dear boy, is far too precious . . .'

'For ninepence I bleedin' am,' mutters Tip, glancing sidelong at Shaw.

Tip's mother looks up from the glass and gasps in horror. 'Ninepence!' she exclaims, clasping the boy protectively to her bosom, dragging his head forcibly across the bar with remarkable ease. The card game stops and falls silent as the entire group turns to watch.

'Ninepence for life and limb! My poor baby! That's done it!' she exclaims. 'Out!'

Ironic cheers from the gaming crowd.

'Milly, my dear woman,' says Shaw, 'don't let's be hasty.'

'You heard the *lady*,' stresses the second clerk, placing his glass down on the bar with a thump.

'My dear boy,' says Shaw, 'she ain't a *lady*, and the day I listen to a young milksop like you . . .'

~

There once was a time when Henry Shaw Esquire could have stood square against a dozen men, or so he would have you believe. Certainly, he is a bulky man with a wide girth and large fists. Nothing more, perhaps, should be deduced from this description, since the combined weight of Milly Lampton's two young admirers is more than sufficient to place him outside the Little White Lion in a horizontal position unsuited to his comfort. He stands up and picks the mud, and worse, from his trousers with the air of a man not entirely unfamiliar with such setbacks. As he is doing so, Bilcher (of Bilcher's Urban Comestibles) exits the Lion in the more customary manner and stops in the doorway of his shop.

'Hallo, Shaw! Not your night is it, eh?' says Bilcher. Perhaps he says it rather too cheerily.

'No.'

'They didn't tell you, did they?' says Bilcher, smiling.

'Tell me what?' snaps Shaw.

'The crushers was round here before, looking for you. Inspector Burton, no less.'

Shaw picks up his hat from the gutter and wonders where he will stay for the night.

It begins to rain.

Tip Lampton leaves the bar and goes up to his room to listen to the rain. He kneels upon the bed, peering through the cloudy glass of his window and surveys the rain-swept street. Harry Shaw has already vanished. In his place, in the alley that runs beside the pub, he notices the usual girl, wrapped in a shawl of peacock colours, her arms braced against the wall. A grim-faced man squirms against her from behind, calico trousers around his ankles, his backside clearly visible as he grunts and groans, shoving her face into the wet bricks with his hand.

Tip watches for a short while, then turns away and pulls the blanket across his body. From the bar, he can clearly make out his mother's laughter and guffaws from the two clerks. As he falls asleep, he wonders how much longer it will be before she struggles up the stairs with one of them in tow.

The rain begins to fall heavier upon the roof. He wakes to hear his mother on the landing, telling the man to be quiet.

CHAPTER SEVEN

WAPPING WALL

ONCE MORE, I am thrown back into the world, feeling like a new-born child.

I walk on, past the police station, through pools of rippling water that reflect the lamps of the riverside taverns: The Scot's Arms, The Tunnel Railway, Thistle and Crown, The Gun Tavern, The White Swan. I know these places, or at least ones like them. Each of these ale-houses has its own distinctive inheritance of dockers and sailors, magnetised together, even in their leisure, by an allegiance to certain wharves or ships. Several groups of these men, ready for their evening spree, pass me by with offers or curses, but, in truth, I can barely see them at all. I cannot shake Ellen from my head, no matter how fast I walk. And yet, in the end, nothing comes of my thoughts but the simple fact that I will need money for lodgings.

I am almost at the end of the High Street when I finally see the familiar trio of gleaming globes above a shop front. The sign reads 'Money

Advanced upon Items of Value. Special Consideration Given to Her Majesty's Navy', and, to leave Her Majesty's Navy in no doubt of its unconditional welcome, a colourful Jolly Jack Tar has been painted alongside. Moreover, a miscellany of maritime relics is laid out in the windows, awaiting salvage by long-forgotten owners: sextants, charts, bronze telescopes, a pair of hammocks, many outlandish items I cannot categorize and all manner of sea-going costumes decorated with anchors and the names of ships. Even as I reach out to try the door, an unkempt little girl swings it open from the inside and, clutching tight a ten-bob note between her fists, scrambles past me and off towards the river. The shop is open, at least.

The interior is lined with glass-fronted cabinets, all ornate rosewood carvings and sparkling with polish, and, to my relief, I see some clothing and household stuff on display in addition to the nautical exhibits. A bald creature, wearing half spectacles and a suit far too tight for his bones, looks up at me from behind the confines of the counter booth and then gazes back down to his books, apparently satisfied that I will not be a nuisance. I suppose that he often sees much worse. He says nothing, and so I undo the mantle I chose from Cave's haul and lay it on the counter underneath his nose.

'Two shillings,' he whispers, without looking up.

He knows it is stolen, of course; it is worth ten times that amount, but I can hardly contradict him. I look around the shop and notice a crumpled red shawl on top of a heap of clothing laid by the door, no doubt recently deposited.

'Done,' I say to him, peeling the shawl from the pile, 'if I might have this thrown in.' It cannot be worth tuppence, and I need something to cover my shoulders.

The bald man raises his eyebrows, dusts the mantle down and tugs at the seams, testing the stitching with his bony fingers. Apparently satisfied, he reaches into the till and silently places two shillings upon the counter. I take the money gladly, wrapping the shawl around my shoulders, and I turn towards the door. As I leave, he comes out from behind the counter and opens the door for me.

'Miss?'

'Yes?'

'Do call again, should you wish to dispose of any further items from your wardrobe.'

He bolts the door behind me.

~

Mother [tearful]: Go and give this clock to your 'uncle'.

Daughter [an innocent]: My 'uncle'?

Mother [exasperated]: The man in the shop with the three balls.

Daughter [confused]: Three balls? Ain't that very awkward?

Jenkins kept that one for the worst gaffs.

~

It is beginning to rain, drizzling on the cobbles and turning the mud into a viscous paste, flushing people into houses and pubs. I feel like I have already been walking for hours, all to no purpose. I notice a potato-seller huddling over his can in one of the warehouse doorways, warming his hands by the coal burner.

'Baked taty?' he shouts, catching my greedy eye. 'Ha'penny to you, Miss.'

I consider, then dart across the road, dodging the worst of the dirt. 'Please,' I say, handing him one of the shillings.

'No pennies?' he says, screwing up his face, examining the coin, biting it for luck.

'I'm sorry.'

'Don't trouble yerself,' he says, digging deep in his pockets for the change. I can see he is looking me up and down, revising his opinion of me as he notices the bruises on my face and the state of my hair. He lifts the lid and stabs out a potato with a toasting fork.

'Careful, it's hot,' he says, wrapping it in a piece of torn newspaper then handing it to me.

'Thank you,' I say, but I clutch it to my chest, welcoming the warmth. 'I'm looking for lodgings. Would you know of anywhere near here?'

The man smiles. 'How particular are yer?'

'Not very,' I reply, in all honesty.

'Mrs. Flanagan's in Prusom Yard is yer best bet. She'll take on anyone, beggin' yer pardon. Turn left at the top and left again.'

I thank him and make a run for it, dodging in and out of doorways, stopping briefly to devour the potato, pulling apart the skin with my fingers.

Lord, I must look a sight.

The rain becomes heavier, and, shawl or not, I'm drenched long before I reach Prusom Yard. It is not so easy to locate as my informant suggested, reached by a narrow alley-way easily missed in the dark. The place itself is the common muddle of bricks and mortar, empty except for a coster's cart and a forlorn donkey, scrambling to find shelter beneath it. I can only be thankful that someone has scrawled the word 'Lodgings' in uneven chalk across one of the doors; I knock as hard as I am able, and a throaty female voice beckons me inside. I push at the door and am welcomed by a gust of hot air that belches out as soon as I open it: the interior itself appears to be a common kitchen and laundry, sweltering with discarded garments drying by the fireplace, generating steam and smoke in equal proportion. Four young women sit on stools around the hearth, chattering to each other and warming their hands, passing a bottle of gin between them. They motion to me to shut the door. A fifth female, buxom and more matronly in appearance, is scrubbing away at a large table top. A quick glance in my direction is enough to satisfy the curiosity of the girls around the fire, and they continue with their talk. The woman at the table, however, quits her cleaning, rubbing her hands dry upon her apron, and walks towards me. She must be forty or more, rosy-cheeked and dark-skinned, with a scruffy frilled cap covering her tousled brown locks.

'Can I help you, dear?' she says.

'Is it Mrs. Flanagan?'

'Well, it's not the Queen of Sheba, bless you,' she cackles. A couple of the others laugh. I try to raise a smile.

'I'm looking for somewhere to stay and was told you take lodgers, Ma'am.'

'Sure enough, dear, sure enough, if you're not too proud to share,' she says, beckoning me to sit down on a bench next to the table. 'Now, first things first, though it's terrible hard of us, I must be asking you straight off for something small in the way of, shall we say, an advance consideration.'

'How much?' I ask. Perhaps I am too blunt.

'You're a sharp one, aren't you, dear? Four pennies a night, one night in advance, penny extra for any gentleman callers. Now, does that suit?'

I agree to the terms and give her the money, which she tucks into the pocket of her apron.

'Now then, dear, my friends call me Annie, and what shall we call you?'

'Flora,' I say, after a hesitation.

'Grand! Flora, now let me be introducing you to our party,' she says, gesturing towards the girls gathered round the fire. 'Now, over there is Jane, she's been with us two months now, a great credit to the house, Lord bless her, and next to her is Sally, a little wonder who joined us last week from out Romford way, isn't that right, my dear? Then we have Dora, who we calls our little Dormouse, God love her, and at the end there is Maggie, who is what I would be calling a close personal acquaintance, having been with us almost six months, is it not, Maggie darlin'?'

Maggie, the older of the four, although I'd say not yet thirty and quite pretty, nods in agreement and turns to me with a quizzical expression.

'That's a precious article what you're wearing.'

'This?' I say, ingenuously, looking down at the shawl.

She ignores me and reaches out towards me, feeling the material of my dress, 'Poplin? You shouldn't 'ave it in the rain, you know. Where d'you buy it?'

'She couldn't 'ave bought it, Mags, must 'ave been a gift from an admirer,' chirrups the one called Jane.

'Nah, you're both wrong, its a family heirloom, ain't it, darlin'?' adds Sally quickly, stroking the cloth like a draper's assistant, laughing out loud. The other one, Dora, just stares at me.

'Now ladies, you've had your fun,' interrupts Mrs. Flanagan, 'and at least Flora here is, be thankful, a paying guest, however she comes by her garments. And how about you, Dor'? I haven't yet seen your doss money today, have I now?'

Dora looks at her feet, but, before Mrs. Flanagan can pursue her remark, the girl has got up and gone out into the rain, shaking her head, muttering that she will be back in a few minutes. Whoops of delighted laughter issue forth from the other three, and I cannot help but ask them what might be so funny.

'Bless you, darlin',' says Maggie, hardly able to contain herself, 'our Dormouse couldn't find a game cove if you stripped her buck naked and planted her in Chelsea Barracks, let alone a wet night round Wapping. She'll be lucky to pull a tuppenny trembler down at St. Kath's, if she don't fall in first.'

'Or jump,' says Sally.

'Or is pushed!' adds Jane, giggling hysterically, finding her own contribution by far the most comical.

'Ladies, ladies,' bellows Mrs. Flanagan, 'whatever will our Flora be thinking? We're all pals here, Flora, I'm sure. Now, we'll be putting you with Maggie there, if that's agreeable. The room's at the top of the stairs and on the left, and you can go up whenever suits. You'll find there's always a basin as is made up for the morning.'

I thank her and go straight upstairs, pleading tiredness and the wet clothes, though I am grateful to get clear of my fellow ladies. The house itself is quite decent, and the room, when all things are considered, is unusually clean, with a dresser in the corner and thick cloth curtains. The bed is more shabby perhaps, narrow planks bedded with straw and rough woollen blankets; at least there is no sign of vermin, nothing larger than a tick or two, and the place is quite dry.

In truth, I ache for sleep. I peel off the damp shawl and the dress and lay them on the floorboards within easy reach, creeping under the covers in my new drawers and chemise. I consider what to do with the remaining coins, still clutched in my hand. In the end I perform the old trick, picking up the dress and making a small tear in the lining of one of the sleeves, dropping them inside.

Heat from the kitchen wafts up the through the floor; I can half hear comings and goings below, more screaming and laughter. I am soon asleep.

~

Where am I now?

The spectators around Tyburn have swollen in numbers to thousands or tens of thousands, all straining their necks to see the scaffold. Many have waited for hours as the July heat soaks up a foetid evaporation of gin and sweat, stinging my throat. My father, visibly tired, hoists me on his shoulders, and it comes as a relief when the cart draws up in procession from Oxford Street. They roar and clap like thunder as the man mounts the steps to the triangular scaffold. Often, the condemned will make a speech, hoping for a delayed pardon or pity from the crowd. This one does nothing.

Except fall.

~

Awake again. Maggie has come in with a candle and is undressing. She unbuttons her frock and slips in beside me without any self-consciousness.

'Don't mind me,' she says, almost bumping me onto the floor.

I can hear her breathing for a while, and then she says, 'Where d'you hail from, Florry?'

'Salisbury,' I reply. That should be far enough.

'Really? It don't sound it. What brings you down here then, darlin'? Fine girl like you, fine dress like that, you should be up the Haymarket out for the toffs. You won't find much quality round 'ere.'

'I'll be moving on soon,' I say, pulling the sheets tight.

Maggie falls silent, apparently happy with this. Then she adds, 'You should have stayed down with us a while. You've missed all the excitement.'

'What's that?' I ask, trying not to sound irritable or uninterested.

'You know the murder, that business with the singer, Ellen wotsername?'

I feel my throat tighten involuntarily.

'Ellen Warwick?'

'That's the one. Well, the Mouse only comes back and tells us the police found a body by Union Stairs . . . they reckon it was that girl what did it, the servant. Drowned herself.'

Not quite, I think to myself, not quite drowned. Not quite a servant.

Chapter Eight

Wapping New Stairs

Daniel Quill *stares* at the dank walls of the cell. Dense moss, sucking up life from the river, holds together the stonework in the approximation of a cube, eight feet square all told. There is one door, thick oak with an iron grille, which swings softly on its hinges, wide open for now. Daniel sits on his chair, back straight, tapping against the small wooden table with his foot, listening to the slosh of the river outside. He is a thin man, six feet tall and quite handsomely dressed, unaccustomed to such surroundings. A splash of footsteps in the corridor outside heralds the appearance of two others. One wears a police sergeant's uniform; the other is dressed in a careworn tweed suit. The former is clearly the elder of the two and has the generous belly of a man well acquainted with the local ale-houses; the other is younger, perhaps thirty five, with a fulsome beard of ginger curls that make extravagant claims for his face. He sits down upon a chair opposite Daniel Quill and offers him a cigar from his jacket pocket, which is silently refused.

'I'm sorry we had to use the basement, Mr. Quill, but all the rooms upstairs are full, you see,' he says, shrugging apologetically and smiling. 'Too many guests.'

The sergeant laughs approvingly and draws out a notebook and pencil.

'Now I've asked Sergeant Johnson here to take notes of our little meeting, Mr. Quill, I hope you have no objections on that score.'

'I object to the fact you've dragged me here at this hour, a second time, on some pretext,' says Quill.

'No pretext, I do assure you, Sir, but rather a highly pertinent development, I should say. I believe we may have found your Miss Meadows.'

'She was never *mine*, Inspector,' says Quill, suddenly blushing despite himself. 'I barely knew the girl . . . Do you mean that you've found her body?'

'Didn't I explain?' intones Inspector Burton, 'My apologies. I mean to say *a* body, which may or may not belong to Miss Meadows. As a matter of fact, I was hoping you might identify the young woman for us.'

'Me?' says Quill, his face draining from red to white.

'Well, we don't believe she had any family to speak of, and you did know her well enough to recognise her, did you not, Sir? Certainly, we'll have to check with someone else of her acquaintance, if anyone can be found, and the man Shaw . . .'

'Once we find him,' interrupts Johnson.

'Indeed, once we find him,' continues the Inspector, 'but I'd be pleased if you could take a look for us, Sir, in the spirit of co-operation.'

Quill bites his lip, then says, 'Very well.'

'Good man! This won't take long. We have her just next door,' says Burton.

'Next door?'

'If you please, Sir. Won't take long, I am sure.'

The sergeant motions them into the passage where they lead Quill at a brisk pace down the corridor to an unmarked cell. The sergeant pulls up his key chain and unlocks the door, taking Quill by the arm and drawing him gently inside.

'If you please, Sir.'

In the centre of the bare chamber, illuminated by the half-light of a single oil lamp, lies a shape, discernibly female, raised upon a low pallet, covered by a shroud of damp mottled cotton. The air stinks of chlorine, and beside this makeshift bier sits a tray of pharmacological bottles, a scalpel and other metal instruments. The sergeant walks round the figure and beckons Quill to stand beside him.

'I apologise for the fumes, Sir,' he says, 'but you wouldn't welcome the alternative, I'll warrant. We had to make some initial anatomical investigations, you see?'

'Are you ready, Sir?' asks Burton, watching him intently.

Quill nods, coughing.

Sergeant Johnson bends down to the pallet and slowly pulls back the sheet like a butcher revealing his finest cuts. The cloth clings to the body like a bruised second skin, adhering to the damp flesh as he gently peels it away. He tugs at it whenever it sticks. Quill, in turn, does not flinch, but fixes his eyes steadily on the material as it comes free, standing mute as a statue.

'It's her.'

'You recognise her as Natalie Meadows? I'm sorry to press the point, Sir, but, with respect to the lady, there isn't that much left to see, is there?' says Burton.

'It's her, damn you!' splutters Quill, half choking.

'Very well, Sir,' says Burton, 'very well. No need to upset yourself. You come back with me and sit down a while. Johnson, get Mr. Quill a nice drop of brandy, and we'll continue our little chat.'

—

'I told you all the facts last time,' says Quill, taking a long swig of pale liquor.

'There's nothing like facts for foxing a gentleman,' suggests the Sergeant. 'Nothing like it. Many a time, I've found facts to be the most misleading information that you might encounter.'

'Sergeant Johnson is not wrong, Sir,' opines Burton. 'Kindly tell us again.'

'For the last time,' says Quill, tetchily, 'I was drinking at the Old Bull, you know that for a fact, and I came back to the house for eleven o'clock or thereabouts . . .'

'Miss Warwick's house?'

'Yes, of course,' snaps Quill. 'I came back and Miss Warwick told me she had been arguing with the Meadows girl. I thought nothing of that and went to bed. I went up the back stairs to my room . . .'

'The attic.'

'Indeed, the attic.' he says, sarcastically. 'You may not be acquainted with this information, Inspector, but you will normally find a servant's quarters in the upper part of a house.'

'I am aware of that, Mr. Quill. Please continue,' says Burton.

'It wasn't long before I heard her scream . . .'

'How long?' interrupts Burton.

'I couldn't say. Fifteen or twenty minutes, maybe less. What does it matter? I heard a scream and ran down the stairs to the parlour. I saw Meadows, standing there, with the blood still on her hands. She ran off before I could even speak. Then I went for the police. That's the end of it. I didn't see anything else. I've already told you all of this, Inspector. May I go now? Frankly, I don't feel well.'

'The girl, did she have a knife?'

Quill sighs. 'I don't know. I do not believe so. She's dead now, Inspector. Really, what does it matter?'

Quill's fingers tap anxiously on the table.

'That's a fine suit, Mr. Quill.'

'Miss Warwick was a good employer, Inspector. She paid good wages.'

'So do the penny papers, eh?' says Burton, cheerily. 'Almost seems like they knew about this before we did.'

Quill blushes. 'As I said, I came straight to the police.'

'Another tack, then. Do you have any idea, Mr. Quill, why Miss Warwick kept no other servants? No cook, for instance?'

'Meadows did some cooking and cleaning, Inspector, as you well know. As to why there was no regular cook or maid, I have no particular idea.'

'You never asked?'

'It would not be my place to ask. And, besides, is it not obvious?'

'Enlighten us, Sir.'

'Miss Warwick was hardly a *lady*, Inspector. How could she place herself above a maid or cook, when she was of the same class?'

'And yet you yourself worked for her...?'

'I had left my previous employer, and I was in need of a situation.'

'And your former employer was the Right Honourable James Aspenn, MP?'

'Yes, Mr. Aspenn. Really, Inspector, if you want my character, you must speak to him yourself.'

'We have. He speaks highly of you, Mr. Quill. Although, I'd say it was a bit of a disappointment for you, was it not? I mean, going from being in the employment of a Member of Parliament to... well, someone like Miss Warwick. One might even call it a little peculiar.'

'Needs must, Inspector. Really, this is becoming tiresome. I would like to go.'

'Very well, Sir, very well. Johnson here will show you out. Again, many thanks for your co-operation. I'm sure you wish to see the culprit apprehended as much as we do.'

'Indeed, good evening to you,' mutters Quill, getting up and storming out well ahead of the Sergeant.

Burton pours himself a glass of the brandy and sips until Johnson returns.

'Do you think he did it?' asks the Sergeant, looking eagerly at his superior.

'Well, I don't believe him,' says the Inspector. 'Do you?'

Daniel Quill walks in the rain and darkness from Wapping High Street. He has barely started when a cab pulls up beside him, keeping pace with him as he walks. A few words are exchanged between Quill and the occupant, but then it stops, and he climbs swiftly inside.

Chapter Nine

Wapping Wall to Old Street

A SOLITARY CAB SPEEDS along in the rain, past the Tower and then Aldgate Pump. Inside sit two men, Daniel Quill and the original occupant of the vehicle, a rather portly man, balding, dressed in a smart evening suit. Both avoid each other's gaze, and Quill shifts uncomfortably in his seat at every bump in the road.

'Your interest in my welfare is rather gratifying, Sir,' says Quill, sarcasm in his voice. 'Second only to that of the police.'

'Would you rather have walked and be soaked to the skin?' replies his companion.

Quill shrugs. 'How did you know I was there?' he asks, after a minute or more of silence.

'I have a passing acquaintance with a man at Scotland Yard.'

'Then why on earth do you wish to talk to *me*?' asks Quill.

'You know very well. Come, be frank. What did you tell them? Did they mention my name?'

'I told them the truth. I was just talking about you, in fact.'

The man appears shocked, turning his reddening face to look at Quill directly. But the latter merely smirks.

'In as much as I told them nothing. For God's sake, I know nothing about it, except that I found her there.'

'So you say.'

'So I say.'

'Do not toy with me, Mr. Quill. I had a profound regard for Miss Warwick . . .'

Quill laughs, a hollow laugh, quite empty of mirth, cutting off the man's speech. 'And you, Mr. Aspenn,' he exclaims, 'are an awful old hypocrite. But you need not worry, I removed every trace of you, rest assured.'

'And you watch your tongue,' replies the man, gripping Quill's arm. 'Remember who I am.'

'What are you? A *respectable* man? A man of honour?' asks Quill, sourly, shaking his arm free of the man's grip but falls silent and stares out of the window. The streets appear unfamiliar for a moment, until he recognises Moorgate.

'Was it the servant? Was it her body they found?' asks Aspenn, breaking the silence.

'I believe so.'

'You are not certain?'

Quill shudders involuntarily as he recalls it. 'I did not care to enquire too closely. She had been in the river for days.'

'Well, then, the matter is done with.'

'Perhaps.'

'How not? Do not cross me, Mr. Quill, I warn you. You may be no longer in my employment, but you do not cross me. This business may turn out badly for all parties, we must toe the same line.'

'It is not me that should concern you. Have you settled matters with Wilkes? He will want more.'

'Well, I will not pay him now. I am bled dry. I have given him the house, after all.'

'That is your business, but I fear it will not be enough for him.'

Again, the two men fall quite silent. It is not long before Quill sees St. Luke's Church and bangs on the roof, bidding the cab to stop.

—

James Aspenn closes the cab door. He watches Daniel Quill scurry through the rain, down the alley that runs by the church. He stares fixedly at him until he disappears from view, but his mind is elsewhere, and it is only when the driver enquires whether he should proceed that he is woken from his reverie. He ponders whether to return home or to Westminster, where a late sitting of the Commons may provide him with a good supper and decent company; indeed, there may be a vote, in which case it is rather his duty to attend. He chooses the latter course and directs the cabman accordingly. Despite this, it is not long before he bids him to pull to a halt again, wheels clattering to a stop beside the corner of Goswell Road, where a young girl, sixteen at best, stands in a doorway, bare-headed and bare-necked, sheltering from the unrelenting rain. She is quite pretty, a round figure and rosy-cheeked, but her shawl and dress are quite unsuited to such weather. Nonetheless, she darts forward to the cab door, a smile fixed upon her face, and is not surprised when it opens to receive her.

'Come,' says Aspenn, 'you'll be getting wet.'

'My,' she says, observing the well-dressed man as she steps up, 'you're a fine gentleman to be stoppin' here.'

'And you, my dear, are very fine indeed,' says James Aspenn, MP. 'How much?'

The girl giggles, letting him fumble with her skirts.

'Whatever do you mean?'

'How much?'

'Five bob.'

—

Daniel Quill hastens along the church path to his father's house. The old man is asleep in the kitchen, so he doesn't disturb him as he climbs quietly to the tiny bedroom that used to make him so miserable as a young man.

He sits down on the bed and pours himself a glass of whisky from the nearby bottle. Ellen Warwick's picture smiles at him from the wall.

He listens to the rain outside and ponders his future, until sleep drags him away.

Chapter Ten

Seven Dials to Shepherdess Walk

Tip Lampton wonders what time it might be, though he knows it is still the middle of the night. He places his rush light upon the windowsill and opens the book he took from Bowles' shop. In the dim light of the room he cannot make out the finer detail of the prints, but he understands them well enough. One girl lies upon a divan draped in silk, her head coquettishly poised on her shoulder; here is another, stretched langourously against a wall; this one squats down; the next one merely stands, clothed only in shadows; the next lies upon her stomach; here is another that leans upon her side. Two dozen pages in all, pose after pose. Even the girls in the street do not parade themselves in this way, everything bared and on display. He will burn it on the fire, he thinks to himself.

He hears his mother moving about in her room, getting rid of the man from earlier, and snuffs out the candle.

—

Harry Shaw leaves behind Seven Dials, pulling his

hat tight over his ears as the rain pours down. He suspects it will be a long night. He decides upon a route through Holborn and Smithfield, visiting a succession of taverns and ale-houses where he hopes to trade upon a past friendship or old favours. As the night progresses, however, he finds himself disappointed at every turn and, in some cases, even made quite unwelcome by his former acquaintances. In desperation, he turns towards Clerkenwell and the City Road, and it is past the stroke of midnight that he stands outside the Eagle tavern, that famous resort of popular amusement. The rain has not yet ceased, and a crowd of dampened revellers huddle, together in the arch of the doorway, recently ejected from the warmth of the tap-room and parlour. They hardly notice as he slips between them and, conjuring a key from deep inside his jacket like the best magician, lets himself in.

During its opening hours, the tap-room of the Eagle is a lavish affair, resplendent in brass fittings, mahogany and gilded glass, thronging with customers and merriment. In the semi-darkness, however, illuminated only by the dying embers of the hearth, the cold golden gleam of the metal only chills the room, and the splendid mirrors simply reflect Shaw's fleeting ghost as he moves between the tables and pillars, leaving a trail of damp footprints upon the floor. Eventually, he eases his way behind the bar, but there is no money box to be found, nor liquor; everything has been locked away. He curses his luck and grapples with the door that leads to the stairs. He ascends them cautiously, testing for creaks with balanced steps, as if very familiar with such manoeuvring, only halting when he spots a door on the second floor that has been left ajar, shedding candlelight upon the landing. He peers inside.

The room is a curious mixture of relics from parlour, kitchen and bedroom, incorporating elements of all three within its cramped confines. A double bed, an upright piano, a small stove, dining table, three armchairs, several battered paintings: everything has been placed, back to back, in a jumbled confusion. Moreover, in the middle of this domestic morass, an old woman slumps in a capacious armchair, snoring in tandem with the small dog cradled in her lap. The light emanates from a silver candlestick that she clutches quite upright in one hand and, as she snorts, each reverberation spills tears of wax onto her apron, measuring out sleep in a bulbous pond. The dog, meanwhile, a French poodle of the smallest proportions necessary for maintaining life, opens one eye. Shaking itself awake, it wriggles free from its mistress and jumps across the debris to sniff Shaw's ankles. He kicks it casually in the stomach, realising his mistake as soon as he does so, for it prompts a piercing yelp sufficient to disturb the old woman from her slumber. The candlestick swings wildly above her head as she springs upright. Fortunately, given the proximity of so many combustible items, the light goes out.

'Spare me!' she shouts hoarsely.

'Shush, you old fool,' hisses Shaw. 'It's me.'

The old woman squints through the blackness. 'Henry?'

'Yes, who else?' mutters Shaw impatiently.

'How should I know, creeping around like that?' says the woman without any hint of feeling, sagging back into the recesses of the chair. 'Where you hiding, Spoonikins? Come to mother.'

The dog makes no answer, cowering by the chimney breast. The old woman, in turn, shoves her hands repeatedly down the folds of her clothes, as if to check she has not inadvertently suffocated the animal. Eventually, she abandons this search and relights the candle, throwing her visitor into flickering definition. He pulls up a chair and sits beside her.

'How have you been, Jemmy?' he asks.

'Where's Spooney? Where is he?' she says, glancing nervously around, seemingly unaware of his question.

'Blast the dog, you old fool,' he says, as a new thought occurs to him now that he is discovered. 'Listen to me. I need a bed for a night or two.'

'Needs the bed now, does he, Spoonikins? Taken everything else, needs the bed now! Ha!'

Shaw watches her with undisguised contempt.

'Doesn't you like him, Spooney? Is that why you're hiding?'

'Blast the dog, I say. Do you even hear me?' he says.

'The Married State. A Sentimental Proposition to be Enacted by Two Parties. Tuppence to enter. One performance only. We liked that, didn't we,

Spoonikins? We liked you then.'

'Have you heard a word I've said?' he says again, raising his voice in frustration.

Before she can speak, a voice comes from the hall. 'She hears you, Harry. I wouldn't doubt it. They can hear you in Hackney Wick, I'd reckon.'

Arthur Wilkes appears at the door with a candle, wearing a nightgown and cap. His face looks even more rodent-like in the half light, his two keen pinprick eyes fixing upon Shaw. Beside him stands a tall muscular man in fustian trousers and a cheap shirt, equally grim-faced. His head is shaven, and the spirals of an intricate naval tattoo peek from under his collar.

Shaw freezes for a moment, then strolls towards Wilkes grinning. 'Brother-in-law! What a coincidence – who's your friend?'

'How did you get in?' asks the Weasel, ignoring Shaw's outstretched hand.

'Now now, Arthur, let's not begin by quarrelling. I believe my lady wife here gave me a key, which I happen to have fortuitously retained when we last parted, nothing more to it.'

'Twelve months ago, Harry, weren't it? I'd like to say we've missed you, but, as you can tell, my sister ain't been herself for a while, not since you "parted", as it happens.'

'She's fine, Arthur, we'll soon perk her up,' says Shaw.

'Ha!' exclaims Jemima Shaw.

'She don't need your sort of help, Harry Shaw, not by a long chalk. This is my junk room, see? Anything you left her with, we put it in here. And she's slept here ever since. I don't know why she's happy staying in here with it, but she is. There ain't much point in adding you to the fixtures, now is there, when you made her how she is?'

Shaw makes no reply to this but looks nervously at the Weasel's burly companion.

'As a matter of fact, Arthur, I am a little down on my luck at the moment, and I was wondering if you could oblige a relative. I was just discussing it with Jem here, and we thought perhaps if I could just stay the night and we could . . .'

'I ain't obliging you with anything pecuniary, Harry, if that's what you're thinking,' says the Weasel. 'I think you should be on your way.'

Shaws ponders the matter and resolves to cut his losses. He makes to leave, but the old woman grabs his sleeve.

'Let him stay, Arthur, won't you?' she says. 'It's been so long since I seen him.'

Wilkes sighs. 'I suppose if Jem don't mind, you might stay one night . . .'

He looks at his sister, hoping that she might object, but she only closes her eyes. Shaw smiles.

'I weren't thinking of charity, Arthur,' Shaw persists. 'You're a man of business these days, what with this place, and I can offer you the benefits of my experience. Perhaps there is some work you could put my way . . . for your nearest and dearest, as it were?'

'Employ you? Here?' The Weasel sneers, wrinkling his thread-like lips at the corners.

'For Jem's sake, Arthur.'

'For Jem's sake you can sleep here this once, but

I very much hope you ain't planning to make yourself a nuisance, Harry, because my friend Simms here wouldn't take it kindly, not at all.'

The man in question smiles a crooked smile, tensing his substantial shoulders and clenching his fists.

'Not at all!' exclaims Shaw. 'I'm appealing to your conscience, Arthur. There must be something you could manage, for old times?'

'I doubt you could appeal to anyone,' says the Wcascl.

Silence. The two men gaze warily at each other as the old woman begins to snore.

'Very well,' says the Weasel after a painfully long interval. 'As it happens, brother-in-law, I do have a few things that need my attention tomorrow. I'll give you five bob if you help me out with a little something, and that's the last we ever see of you? You won't take to bothering her no more?'

'Ten and you have my word, Arthur, upon my honour.'

The old woman splutters awake.

'Ha!'

Chapter Eleven

Prusom Yard

Where am I?

I float above the sunset Thames, gliding like a gull past countless bridges of glass and iron, floating down to the water's edge by the Tower. The mud is like dough beneath my feet, malleable and warm, cooking in the dying light. A man taps me on the shoulder: he is old and whiskered, though smart in a black suit and silk hat, and he smiles at me as he unbuckles his belt, folding his trousers over three times and laying them down upon the mud. He steps backwards into the river; brown water swirling around his naked body as he slips beneath the surface. When he is gone, I see a silver watch shining in the dirt, the hands slowly revolving backwards.

No, that's not right at all. Where am I?

A new day. I wake up to a cold and empty room, shrouded in shadows. Maggie has disappeared, and I am left alone to clamber out of bed. I scramble into my dress, then find the basin on the dresser and splash my face with brackish water. As I walk out onto the landing, I notice a cracked mirror pinned to the wall; I cannot resist pausing to contemplate the unfamiliar jigsaw of my reflection.

'You're a vain one, ain't you now?' says Mrs. Flanagan, appearing suddenly from the hallway.

'N-no,' I mumble, jumping back.

'Ah, come on now, I was only teasing! Will you not come down and have some bread?'

'Do you know the time?' I ask, descending the stairs and following her into the kitchen.

'Midday or thereabouts,' she says, seating herself at the dining table. No-one else is there except for the younger girl, Dora, who sits solemnly by the fire.

'Now,' resumes Mrs. Flanagan, 'I'm afraid I must be asking for today's money, though it pains me to be so bold.'

She does not look to be in pain.

'No, that's quite fine,' I say, lying. I feel for the coins inside my sleeve, pulling them out. It's only when I finally retrieve them that I realise what's missing: at least a shilling. I apologise and run back upstairs to check the room. Nothing there. No wonder Maggie was up and out so quickly. I should know better.

'Lost something, dear?' says Mrs. Flanagan on my return, taking my four pennies.

'No, nothing of value,' I reply, calmly.

'You should be more careful,' she says, curling her lips. I'd be tempted to slap her, if she were not twice my size.

'Now,' she continues, 'I'm looking at you, Flora, and, I have to say, Lord bless you, you don't look fit for anything, not in the state you're in. We can't do much about the dress, but shall we have a go at your hair? We've got some water on the boil, and I can lend you a fine bar of soap.'

My hair feels like straw and undoubtedly it looks worse. 'Free?' I ask.

'My, you're sharp, young lady, sharp as a pin!' exclaims Mrs. Flanagan, clucking to herself. 'Free to you, my dear, as being our new guest. How does that sound?'

I nod and munch some bread while Dora retrieves a steaming basin from beside the hearth, places it on the table, then goes off again, returning with a jug and a rough bar of soap. I thank her and stoop over the basin, soaking the long strands hesitantly, closing my eyes and running my fingers through and through. I don't think my hair has ever been this long before. Dora hands me the soap, and I just manage to work it through before the door bangs open, wafting cold air through the room. Someone enters, and, though my eyes are closed, I can hear a man's voice.

'Now there's a sight for sore eyes. Do you have a new one, Mrs. F.?'

The voice is rich and polished, a mild Scots accent. I rush to finish washing.

'She's called Flora,' says Dora, giggling nervously.

Mrs. Flanagan mutters something and begs the man to sit down. Dora hands me a cloth, and I dry myself, opening my eyes to look at the new arrival, a short, stocky fellow with pitch-black hands and an unshaven face. He looks like he has seen better days, but I suppose he might say the same of me.

'May I call you Flora, Miss?' he says slowly, exaggerating the courtesy.

'You may call me what you like.'

Dora smiles, steps behind me and, unasked, begins to comb my hair. I wonder if she did find her doss money last night or whether it suits Mrs. Flanagan to keep her as an unpaid servant. Mrs. Flanagan, meanwhile, is gazing at the man with an adoring concentration that almost makes me pity him.

'Well?' Mrs. Flanagan asks him eagerly.

'Is it news you're wanting, Mrs. F.?' he asks with a rhetorical air. 'I have more news than Winged Rumour itself, as the Poet might say.' The man opens a carpet bag he has already laid on the floor and retrieves a bundle of pamphlets and sheets. I see now that it isn't the average London dirt on his hands but printer's ink, layers of block capitals and narrow type smudged into illegible grime.

He coughs and recites from one of the sheets. '"The Shocking Death of Doctor Mallory, Apprehended Atop the Bloody Corpse of his Lover?"'

'Lord no!' exclaims Mrs. Flanagan with enthusiasm.

'We had that one last week,' whispers Dora in my ear, still combing diligently.

'"Dreadful Divulgations from Scotland Concerning Relations between the Prince Consort and Her Majesty?"'

'Ah no, not again,' says Mrs. Flanagan.

'Very well, you leave me no choice but to disclose the latest sensation as yet unseen by the discerning literary public . . .'

'Go on, go on,' says Dora.

'"The Broken Butterfly: Mysterious Murder of Miss Ellen Warwick, as Recounted in Full Detail by her Faithful Manservant Daniel Quill."'

'Manservant?' spits Mrs. Flanagan. 'Murderer more like!'

'They've found the maid, drowned,' whispers Dora to me.

'Are you familiar with the terrible circumstances, Flora?' says the man, grinning at me and pushing a sheet of paper under my nose. 'There's a picture for you.'

He probably imagines I cannot read. The engraving is a stock scene of a mangled corpse, tastefully stretched out, looking no more like Ellen than the Queen herself. He looks surprised when I casually put it aside.

'Never mind her,' says Mrs. Flanagan, looking at me disdainfully, 'I'll take it: Sally can read it out for us later, a regular scholar is our Sally.'

The man smiles at me as he accepts Mrs. Flanagan's penny and leaves the sheet in Dora's hands. She stares at it, cheerily aghast.

'Do they know who did it?' I ask him.

'No, though I've heard they reckon it was the maid – drowned herself, you see. Could not face the rope, you see.'

'They are certain of that?' I ask.

The man shrugs.

'Good for business, is it not?' says Mrs. Flanagan, nudging him, 'and perhaps you'll be back later to see Sally?'

'Ah no, not tonight, Missus. I've got to collect the new sheets we're printing for after the funeral. The fellows are working double-time on the press. Maybe tomorrow. You'll be wanting a copy, I expect?'

Mrs. Flanagan smiles at him pleasantly and confirms she will take a copy. It takes a while for his words to register.

'Funeral? I mean, Miss Warwick's funeral?'

'Well, he hardly meant the Duke of Wellington, did he, dear?' says Mrs. Flanagan, annoyed at my interruption. The man, however, laughs.

'You're not thinking of attending, Flora? It's going to be getting terrible crowded by now.'

'By now? It's today?'

'Aye, today at Abney Park,' he says.

Of course. Where else? I put on my shawl and run outside into the yard, leaving behind all three of them open-mouthed. The man, however, runs to the door and shouts after me.

'There's no hurry, Miss! You won't get in without a ticket! Unprecedented public demand! Pos-it-iv-ely her last performance!'

CHAPTER TWELVE

SHEPHERDESS WALK TO SEVEN DIALS

DAYLIGHT PEERS HESITANTLY through Tip Lampton's window as he places the book upon the newly lit fire. He does not watch as the pages blacken and flare. Instead, he gazes at a crumpled piece of card clutched in his hand.

'Look at her any more and you'll wear it out,' says his mother, appearing in the doorway. 'Ain't you ready? Don't you want us to find a good spot?'

Tip shrugs, and, in turn, his mother frowns and walks to the fireplace to stand beside him. She is dressed in black for mourning and bends down to touch his cheek.

'Ain't you keen to go?'

'I suppose.'

'Well,' she replies patiently, 'you won't get another chance.'

Tip looks at the picture of Ellen Warwick upon the card, the photograph which she handed him herself.

'Don't you want to see her off?' says Milly.

'I'm coming,' he says.

Harry Shaw falls out of bed. The thump of his plump flesh banging against the floorboards is unnoticed by his ageing spouse, who continues to snore, blissfully unconscious, in the embrace of her comfortable chair. As for Mr. Shaw, it takes him some moments, amidst the clutter of Wilkes's abandoned furnishings, to pinpoint his location. In the end he curses under his breath and levers himself vertical against the side of the bed, locating his jacket and boots. With this accomplished, he stumbles between the assorted household obstacles to find the curtains and opens the sash window onto the noisy bustle of the City Road traffic. The steady rumble of wagons and drays, pounding the macadamised road below, reverberates through the room.

'Wake up, woman,' he says tetchily, prodding his erstwhile mate with an outstretched finger. Jemima oscillates in her seat like a provoked jelly.

'Are you deaf as well as stupid?' he enquires, bending down to her ear lobe.

She opens one eye and stares silently at his nose.

'Where do I find Arthur?' he asks.

She looks at him blankly but waves her hand in the direction of the door, gesticulating towards the right. Shaw says nothing in return but leaves the room in search of his benefactor. He finds his brother-in-law downstairs in a narrow box room at the end of the corridor, sitting alone at a sloped desk that speaks more of a lowly clerk than the proprietor of the Eagle Tavern. Nevertheless, there he squats, surrounded by correspondence and contracts, sifting through them with a determined air. Before Shaw can speak, he turns to face him.

'Good morning, Harry. Up with the lark, is it?'

'I could hardly sleep in that room,' mutters Shaw.

'Guilty conscience?'

'You're a comic, ain't you, Arthur? Now how about what we were discussing last night?'

'Very practical of you to remember, Harry, very proper. Well, I'm going to be busy today on some business of a delicate nature, and, in the meantime, I require a letter delivered to a rather select acquaintance. Would that suit?'

'I'm too old to be a delivery boy, Arthur.'

'It's all that's going. Take it or leave it. I'd send Simms, but I need him here.'

'Well,' says Shaw, as if displaying considerable generosity of spirit, 'for Jem's sake, I suppose I can oblige.'

'Yes. I suppose you can,' says Wilkes, opening a drawer in his desk and retrieving an envelope. 'It's very straightforward. Deliver this to the gentleman: I've written the address on the envelope. Make sure he's at home, and wait for a reply. Come back here tonight at, shall we say, seven o'clock? Nothing could be easier, I'm sure. The reply's the thing, mind, make sure he reads it. Tell him I sent you.'

'What do I do if he ain't there?'

'Then wait.'

Shaw takes the envelope, and, immediately, the Weasel turns back to his work.

'And the money?' says Shaw uneasily.

'Really, Harry, what do you take me for? Payment upon completion, not a penny beforehand. Do close the door on your way out.'

Shaw frowns and looks around the office. 'How did you come by this place, Arthur? You were selling penny postcards in the street when I married her, weren't you?'

The Weasel smiles. 'There's profit even in that, if you knows where to look, like with anything. Now, look at yourself, Harry, happy to run errands for a couple of bob. Who would have thought it? Now, are you off, or should I call Simms?'

Shaw looks at him, and, initially, he seems about to argue, perhaps even grow angry. However, if this resolution is present, it soons crumbles, and, biting his tongue, he tucks the envelope inside his jacket as he makes his way downstairs. The bar is still as empty as when he entered the previous night, and so he heads for the kitchen, hoping, at the very least, to breakfast on some left-overs. Unfortunately, even such culinary delights are unattainable, since the larder is locked, and, though he makes every effort to peruse the cupboards, he obtains nothing more than a passing intimacy with assorted pots and pans. Abandoning this fruitless search, he sits down by the kitchen table and takes the envelope out of his pocket, laying it down in front of him. *25 Manchester Square*. He holds it up to the light like a scientific curiosity, fingering the seal with grubby hands, leaving black smudges on the cream paper. Nothing, however, can be seen of the contents, and, wary of being found, he moves on, replacing it in his pocket and making his way back through the bar and, finally, out once again onto the street.

The rain has stopped, but the mud is ankle-deep on the City Road. Every inch is congested with horse-drawn vehicles, all plodding placidly forwards. Brewers' drays swing out into the traffic towards the Angel, a crowded omnibus creeps towards Moorgate, passengers shivering on the open deck. Only the City clerks move at any pace, whole offices of men walking briskly from the heights of Holloway and Islington, each one engaged in solitary contemplation of his own feet and, at suitable junctures, the adjustment of a stovepipe hat. They hardly notice Shaw as he meanders across the road towards the smoking manufactories of Clerkenwell and, in all fairness, he barely notices them but for the occasional watch or tie-pin that gleams in the light, begging him to be relieved of its owner, teasing his once-nimble fingers. Instead, however, he walks in the direction of Holborn, wandering through the streets of Clerkenwell and up the tumbling incline of Snow Hill, stopping only to purchase a hot muffin from a passing tray, worsening his diminishing finances by a ha'penny. He turns his step onwards to Seven Dials, and, an hour after his departure from the Eagle, he finds himself outside the Little White Lion, a poor imitation of that former establishment but infinitely dearer to his heart. As he arrives, he chances upon the worthy proprietress and her son about to quit the front door and march down the street. Both are dressed in black, and the diminutive Mrs. Lampton is particularly spectacular in a capacious black bonnet and matching muff, which unite almost to conceal her very existence but for the occasional shifting of her skirts and the projection of her imperious chin.

'Hallo, Milly.'

'Well, if it isnt Mr. Shaw. I can't imagine what Mr. Shaw is wanting, can you, Tip?'

'No, Ma. I can't cither.'

'Come on now, Milly, don't be like that.'

'And how do you expect a body to be, when you bring their one and only boy back home trampled by wild animals and Lord knows what else he's suffered? And I suppose you've forgotten what day it is?'

'Saturday?'

'The funeral, Miss Warwick's funeral,' she says irascibly. 'You said you'd come with us, didn't you? You know how she was Tip's favourite. I thought you'd be interested. So much for that. I don't think you give two figs for the boy nor me, I really don't.'

Mrs. Lampton rubs her eyes and trembles around her lips in the most delicate and becoming fashion. One might mistake this for tears.

'Well, hang on, Milly. What's the hurry? I'll just pop in and get the suit and . . .'

'Oh no you don't, Harry Shaw,' interrupts Milly, 'not until I see an apology . . . and I don't mean a few well-chosen words.'

'You're a hard woman, Milly. You never told

me about the bloody police neither. Bilcher said they were looking for me.'

'No, I never did, you're right. Come on, my dear,' she says to the boy.

'Yes, Ma,' replies Tip dutifully as they stroll off.

Harry Shaw waits until they are gone and takes out the letter from his pocket. He toys with the idea of simply opening it but, instead, turns around and walks briskly towards Oxford Street. Perhaps with the five bob he will buy her a present.

CHAPTER THIRTEEN

STOKE NEWINGTON

I SHOULD BE IN mourning.

Crepe and bombazine, jet stones set in silver, black favours in my hair.

I can hear the noise as I walk through Shacklewell Green, the babble of voices and the clatter of boots. It is only when I leave the path by the brick fields and turn onto the broad sweep of the High Street that I can see it: dozens of people, all trudging north in dribs and drabs, many in full mourning dress. Even the shops are shuttered and garlanded with swathes of black crape.

I mingle with the throng and find myself next to a gang of mechanics, dirty from a morning's work and stinking of smoke and beer. They are talking about Ellen, each with his own idiotic theory concerning her death; they seem to find the speculation a great source of entertainment. I restrain an urge to tell them they are fools.

Despite the crush, I manage to excuse myself through the mob as far as the corner opposite the

Three Crowns on Church Street. I garner ripe comments about my dress as I go along, and I cannot blame them, since even the humblest labourer has something, a black armband or neckerchief, some small token of grief. A solid wall of policemen, meanwhile, lines the road on both sides, pushing back the crowd so that they are squeezed tight into every doorway. I find that I am just in time. As the chatter diminishes to an expectant hush, the funeral cortège appears further up the street, rolling into view with stately ceremony and conducted by a professional mute, a tall man in black silk with a dour face and wilting eyes, an expert in directing sorrow. Four proud plumed horses, mimicking his sombre steps, pull the hearse behind him, the usual carriage of glass and gilding. Inside lies the dark wooden coffin, supported on brass rails and bedecked with a mountain of ostrich feathers. It is hard to imagine her lying inside it. I put the thought away. Then comes a single mourners' coach, although I cannot make out the passengers and, lastly, two dozen individuals on foot, people she knew from the theatres and penny palaces: people I used to know myself, Jenkins at their head. The crowd watch mesmerised, many of them crying. The procession, meanwhile, turns left onto the High Street and, for an instant, I can make out the single occupant of the mourners' coach.

Arthur Wilkes.

We wait until an order is given, and the police break ranks, letting the crowd surge after the cortège, running up to the twin obelisks that guard the main entrance to the cemetery. The iron gates have already shut behind the last of the official mourners, and the hearse is disappearing down the long tree-lined avenue that leads to the chapel. The rest of us seem to hold our breath and stare silently at the ironwork, as if expecting a final curtain call. Yet, when this vigil is not rewarded, quiet conversations begin afresh and grow louder. The mass of people gradually begins to thin out, and many of them ask after the nearest public house. Only a few of the most devoted remain by the gates, clasping the bars, in mute pleading for admittance.

Arthur Wilkes? Why on earth Arthur Wilkes?

I wander disconsolately back down Church Street, to see the house for one last time. It is a morbid impulse, I suppose, but better than doing nothing. Still, I cannot cry. I feel only numb. As I reach the old church, two small boys, neatly dressed in black, run up to me carrying a bundle of paper.

'Memorial song sheet of the Butterfly, Miss? Only a penny?'

I ignore them and they soon move on, working their way through the straggling groups of would-be mourners.

The villa itself looks pretty as ever, beside the stream of the New River, the white stucco and black railings reflected in the steady flow of the water. There are little groups of spectators gathered on the bank like black crows, nodding their heads and talking in low tones, the sort who would gape at any spectacle, alive or dead. As I draw closer, some of them begin to tut to each other, and, initially, I assume it is disgust either at my inappropriate attire or my appearance in general. Then I see the true cause of their disapproval: a girl dressed in a white linen gown, quite plain and pallid herself, moving between the cliques of men and women with a handful of leaflets. Behind her, a corpulent young man is busying himself erecting a new sign upon the gates.

Revd. Wallace's Tabernacle of Hygienic Christianity. 15 Paradise Row, Stoke Newington.

'Please, do take one of these,' says the ashen-faced girl, appearing abruptly beside me and offering one of her sheets.

'No, not for me, thank you, really.'

'No-one,' she says, clutching my hands fervently, 'no-one is beyond salvation. Come tomorrow.'

I wince, but she has already moved on through the crowd, many of whom are rather more vociferous than myself in refusing her attentions. Even so, she has managed to leave one of her leaflets crushed between my fingers.

The Society For the Propoundment of Hygienic Christianity
The Revd. Hengist Wallace will give his views
on the meaning of Christian Cleanliness
at the new Tabernacle, 15 Paradise Row, Stoke Newington,
Midday, Sunday 4th February
All welcome

I keep moving, making my way back over Paradise

Bridge, following the river once again to Green Lanes, planning how I might start afresh. And yet, everything feels unfinished.

A distant bell chimes three times, the chapel bell announcing her interment.

Poor Ellen.

Chapter Fourteen

Shoreditch to Brick Lane

How did all this begin?

It began not long after I invented Natalie Meadows.

Natalie, Flora. What is in a name, after all?

I was working in a slop-shop near the Whitechapel Road, doing needlework by the piece; it was tiring work and paid very little, no more than a few shillings a week, depending upon demand. I had been there for only a week or two, and I resolved to spend my free Sunday either at education or leisure. I had no friends to speak of and no money, and so, on the Sunday evening, I found myself seated at the inaugural meeting of the Shoreditch Choral Society. I had seen the advertisements flyposted upon various walls and thought I might attend, since there was no charge for admission, and the church would be warm. As it turned out, there were very few other women present and hardly a man under the age of forty, the only exception being the curate himself, a whey-faced young gentleman of unedifying odour. Indeed, it was a rather godly affair, and I was toying with the idea of departure when an attractive solitary woman of about thirty years sat next to me with a bump. I must have looked quite startled.

'Sorry, darlin', did I scare you?' she asked.

I turned, ready to say something clever, but she was already smiling benignly at me, eyes gleaming.

'No,' I replied, 'I'm sorry, I was day-dreaming.'

'Don't fret,' she replied, peering along the pews. 'My name's Ellie, by the way.'

'How do you do?'

'It don't look very promising, do it?'

'How do you mean?'

'Well, it ain't exactly a lively affair.'

'No,' I said.

The first hymn began and neither of us spoke for the rest of the evening, since she began to converse quite confidentially with a man who sat next to her, though I gathered he was as much a stranger to her as I was. In all fairness, I noted even then that she had a good voice, much superior to mine, but nothing more was said between us.

In fact, our acquaintance would have ended that night had we not happened to live but a few streets apart, in lodgings off the Whitechapel Road. I had barely left the church when she spotted me in the distance, though I had striven to leave the assembly as early as possible. When she discovered where I lived, I could hardly refuse her companionship upon the walk home. I soon realised, however, that, although I might have struggled to make a conversation with anyone else, with Ellen there was no need to make the smallest effort. Taking my arm, she talked at length about herself, her youth (she was an orphan) and her opinions upon every triviality of fashion, music and theatre (for she proclaimed herself 'devoted' to all three). I doubt she learnt anything about me at all that night.

She only paused when we came to the Brick Lane Mansion, a converted public house that dominated that thoroughfare, though not open on a Sunday. There she halted us and bid me gaze up at the newly painted signboard upon the exterior, where a playbill was posted.

'Ain't that a sight!' she exclaimed. I looked at the bill, but could not make out the cause of her delight.

The Seven Steps to Sin, or
The Devil Takes the Hindmost;
Jim Crow, Six Comic and Sentimental Songs;
The Fisherman's Daughter, or
A Tale of Blood

'There!' she said, laughing but clearly annoyed with my incomprehension, pointing at the tiny narrow type squeezed between the first play and the nigger minstrel. I peered closer.

'Miss Ellen Warwick.'

She flushed with excitement as she read out the words.

'You?' I asked. I probably sounded rather supercilious.

'Of course,' she replied. 'And, now we're pals,

you must come and see me. You will come, won't you?'

Before I could draw breath, she told me that she had already appeared at several of the penny gaffs around Whitechapel and the Ratcliff Highway and, to hear her tell it at least, had been greeted with much acclaim.

In the end, I agreed to go and see her the following night. If nothing else, it was the only way to silence her.

I spent the next day working, as usual, amidst piles of cloth and thread, hunched in an ill-lit room with a dozen others, each woman as miserable at her work as myself. I finally escaped at seven o'clock and ran back to my lodgings to change into my other dress, which, although only a dirty cotton smock, at least did not reek of the slop-shop. Ellen had agreed to meet me outside the Brick Lane Mansion, which, she had assured me, as it was a relatively new construction, was much superior to the existing Whitechapel blood-tubs and penny gaffs. I was not confident in this, nor that I could rely on her remembering our arrangement but I found her waiting outside the doors.

'You came!' she shouted, gleefully, as I approached. 'Was no-one else interested?'

'No,' I replied blushing. 'I'm sorry.'

I remembered that I had not fulfilled a promise I had made to 'bring my friends', as if I had a coterie of admirers I could call upon.

'Don't be a goose . . . Come in with me,' she

said, linking her arm around mine and leading me into the cavernous interior where, despite her protestations to the manager, I was still obliged to pay for my ticket. I had to agree with her that the stage was rather handsome for Whitechapel. It was, in fact, raised a good three feet above the ground and blessed with a large painted backdrop, a canvas depicting Alpine mountains and lakes. There were even makeshift private boxes set up on either side, each supported by an ingenious system of platforms and stilts. And yet, for all that, the stalls were much as I had expected, reeking of cheap gin and echoing with raucous laughter from the usual low crowd: gangs of young lads and labouring men, and frowsy women parading themselves for hire.

'What do you think?' she asked me breathlessly, her face illuminated with sheer delight at being there.

'Wonderful,' I replied. I tried to sound sincere. I doubt she even heard me.

'I've got to go and get ready . . . Can you find yourself a seat?'

I said that I could and let her go, but in truth I did not relish the thought of sitting there on my own. Nevertheless, I found a spot towards the back and waited.

It was the fashion, in the penny theatres at that time, to have a drama first on the bill, then a singer or some comic business, and then another drama to finish. The first piece of the night, entitled 'The Seven Steps to Sin', was already well in progress when we entered, though not to any great acclaim. The caperings of several painted devils had plainly done little to appease the crowd, and the male portion of the audience, though it was a mixed house, was more concerned with gaining an unobstructed view of the aisles, where girls strolled up and down in procession. Some of these were no doubt genuine whores, some merely dollies; all were to be had for a shilling or two.

I kept my eyes, therefore, fixed firmly upon the play. In due course the players proceeded to 'a remote fastness in the Italian Mountains' and 'The Infernal Powers at Bay'; it was not a gripping piece by any chalk. In desperation, they began to lavish erruptions of offal upon the stage, intended, as much as I could gather, to graphically illustrate the 'Torments of the Damned'. This stirred some interest in the wider audience, and, after much toing and froing, the ineffectual demons were slain to unanimous approval, amidst more blood and guts and a brief hail of oranges and farthings, the latter intended more to wound than to reward.

I wondered when I might expect to see my new acquaintance. As they began to clear the rubbish from the platform, a sweaty boy of sixteen years or so had separated from his fellows and slunk along the bench next to me.

'You're a pretty one, darlin'. How would you like it?' he whispered, laying his warm hand on my thigh. 'How much?'

I prised his fingers from my leg and pinched him hard. 'Priceless.'

Ellen had appeared from the wings onto the

stage. The boy scowled and let his fingers wander back.

'No need for that, love,' he said. 'Be agreeable. I've got the money.'

Ellen was now centre stage, in a white silk dress that did not quite fit, which I later discovered she had borrowed from the theatre. A piano started on the refrain of a song, which I half knew, and she smiled gingerly as she began to sing, performing a little dance as she went along. She was clearly nervous, and, though I barely knew her, my heart sank when some of them began to jeer at her, shouting obscenities. I remember thinking that if she could just reach her first chorus then the piano might drown them out and carry her through to the end.

It was then it happened.

I was rather preoccupied peeling back the fingers of my juvenile lover, but I still heard the commotion. In fact, although I did not actually see her fall, I heard her slip, the scratch of her shoes scuffing the stage and the swish of the dress as she fell. The piano played on madly for what seemed like a few seconds, and the rambling chords echoed about the hall. I jumped up, and Ellen herself could just be seen rolling on the floor, swaying as she tried to get up, her dress stained with streaks of dark-red gore, which the stage-hands had neglected to remove, looking more like a butcher's apron than a costume. The rest of the hall erupted: even the boy ceased pestering me and convulsed with laughter.

Indeed, it seemed an age before she recovered

her senses. She clambered unsteadily to her feet and, for some unknown reason, curtseyed as she limped from the stage. The audience laughed even harder. I had never felt quite so sorry for anyone.

I got up and went back to the entrance to obtain directions to the dressing room. It was little more than a closet and filled with other people preparing for the second half. I found Ellen there, trying in vain to remove stains from her borrowed dress with a damp cloth. Her arm was bruised, but she was not in the low spirits that I had expected.

'Well,' she said, beaming at me as if nothing had happened, 'it could have been worse.'

—

I think I was her friend from that moment, since I went back to see her perform the next time, and the time after that, until it became a habit. And, in each instance, I thought more highly of her. There was some undefinable quality which she possessed in abundance. It was neither beauty nor talent, though she had something of both, nor did I ever change my opinion of her vanity, or self-absorption. She had, rather, a kind of marvellous self-assurance, a certainty of purpose, which I have never possessed and always find quite astonishing in others.

I used to think that no-one could best her.

Poor Ellen.

CHAPTER FIFTEEN

MANCHESTER SQUARE TO SEVEN DIALS

JAMES ASPENN, MP, stands in his bedroom and watches the clock which sits upon his desk. He is dressed in mourning, a rich cloth suit with black velvet lapels, his hat and cane beside him on the chair. It strikes twelve noon. A few seconds pass and there is a knock on the door. A male servant enters bearing a glass of whisky, which he takes and downs in one swift draught.

'I will change to my day clothes now.'

'You aren't going out, Sir?' asks the footman.

'No. She will be in the ground by now.'

The footman is clearly puzzled, but does not reply, and leaves to fetch the suit.

James Aspenn ponders what to do with the remainder of his day, now Ellen Warwick is dead and buried.

Henry Shaw takes his time walking down Oxford Street, admiring the latest fashions. Many of the shops are open, and he enjoys looking in the windows and considering what effect a well-placed brick might have on the glass. It is nearly lunchtime before he finally makes his way to the well-preserved splendour of Manchester Square. In fact, he dislikes the West End, feeling strangely disorientated amidst such well-planned spaces. Moreover, it takes him some time to find the place on Wilkes's envelope, since many of the residents disdain the use of numbers, and the square itself is empty of anyone who might condescend to offer him advice, not even a crossing sweep. The property turns out to be no more than an average size for the area, with four storeys, five windows on each and no obvious ostentation beyond the painted railings that separate it from the street. He is glad, nevertheless, to find the tradesman's entrance away from public view, and, plucking up his resolve, he firmly bangs upon the knocker.

Nobody answers. He takes the envelope in his hand and reads the name once more: *The Right Honourable James Aspenn.* He tries again and, just as he reaches for the door, it opens. A kitchen maid, or some similar skivvy, stands before him, wiping dirty hands on her apron.

'Sorry, no knives need sharpening, no repairs neither,' she says bluntly, making to close the door. Shaw interjects his hand, stopping her.

'This isn't a casual visit, young lady. I have an especial missive for your master, if he's at home. Would you be so good?' He offers her the envelope, grubby from his fingers.

'Who do you think you are?' she says, giggling.

'Just take it, girl. I'll wait for a reply.'

The girl stops laughing, half-amused and half-perplexed, and takes the letter, closing the door behind her. A few minutes later the door is reopened by an older woman, round and cherubic, splashed with daubings of flour and pastry, no doubt the cook of the house. She holds the letter in her hand, unopened.

'Who are you?' she asks.

'Madam, my name is Shaw, but that ain't material. That letter is an urgent note for your good master, and, I'm afraid, I must await a reply.'

'Ain't you heard of the penny post?' she says, eyeing the offending piece of correspondence with suspicion.

'As I say,' he says tetchily, 'I need a reply.'

'You're all the same. You come here with your bleedin' petitions. This ain't right, that ain't right. Never done a day's work in your life . . .'

She pulls an encrusted lump of pastry free from her blouse and nibbles it, with no particular sense of urgency.

'It is not a petition,' says Shaw, stressing every word as if addressing a small child. 'It's-a-note-for-Mr.-Aspenn-and-needs-a-reply. I'll be waiting here.'

The woman huffs to herself and disappears, shutting the door with a bang. After a few minutes, she returns and leaves him in the company of a stocky young man dressed in the formal green livery of a footman, still holding the unopened letter.

'What do you mean by this?' he asks, waving the envelope under Shaw's nose. 'Who's it from?'

Shaw sighs. '*I* don't mean anything. I'm

delivering it as personal favour for an acquaintance, a Mr. Wilkes. If you'd just take it up to his Lordship, then we could all get on with our business.'

'What's in it?'

'My dear boy, how on earth would I know?'

The footman looks troubled but says nothing more and, once again, closes the door. Shaw leans against the wall and waits with as much patience as he can muster, unused to such delays. Idly, he peers in at the kitchen window, admiring the cook as she retrieves an impressive pie from deep inside the range. Somebody closes the shutters. At least a quarter of an hour passes before the footman returns.

'Well?' asks Shaw.

'Mr. Aspenn would like to see you in person. Wipe your boots and follow me.'

Shaw wipes his boots on the scraper and follows him into the kitchen, attempting to affect a nonchalant air but, in truth, trailing up the stairs in a daze, mentally tallying the market price of every ornament and fitting, in case he should ever have the opportunity to become more closely acquainted with them. He has never been in a house this size; even the carpeting in the hall would buy the White Lion twice over.

Finally, they reach a small room on the first floor, which serves as a library. Every wall is dominated by tall cabinets of books and journals, most of them bound and aligned in smart rows, boastful of expensive subscriptions. There is also a single sturdy armchair, upholstered in leather, but it lies empty. Instead, the Right Honourable James Aspenn, stands by the fireplace, nervously stoking it with a poker. His face is quite red from standing beside the flames.

'Did you bring this?' he asks abruptly, swinging the poker towards Shaw in one hand, waving Wilkes's envelope in the other.

'The letter? Yes, Sir, I did that.'

'And . . . and what right have you, eh?' says the man, dropping the poker into the grate and repeatedly smoothing the creases in his waistcoast. 'What right have you to bring such . . . filthy impertinence into my house? Tell me that!'

'I'm just passing on a note for Mr. Wilkes, Sir, nothing more intended, I'm sure.'

'Nothing more intended? Indeed! Well, do you have this "particular item" on your person? How do I know it exists?'

'What item?'

'Don't play games with me, man. Do you have it or do you not?'

Shaw shakes his head in puzzlement. 'I honestly don't know what you mean, Sir.'

'Oh, really? Well, perhaps you will understand this. You tell your wretched master, tell Mr. Wilkes, that I will have nothing whatsoever to do with him or his sordid requests. Tell him that, and see how he likes it! Tell him that I am bled dry, and there is nothing he can do to change that!'

'I'll do that, Sir,' replies Shaw, uncertain how to proceed.

Aspenn looks equally flustered and thrusts the letter back into Shaw's fingers. 'You can take this and shove it down his wretched throat. I want nothing of it. Nothing more intended indeed! Goodman,' he says, addressing the footman, 'remove this fool from my property.'

Shaw attempts to object to this description, but the footman has already spun him around and on towards the stairs. Before he knows it, a second man is assisting his departure, and, between them, they swiftly have him back outside the tradesman's entrance. Mindful of the previous night, Shaw resigns himself to offering no resistance.

'Cut it, then!' exclaims the footman, making certain explicit gestures at odds with the formality of his dress.

'Charmed, I am sure,' replies Shaw, bowing ironically but, all the same, hurrying on his way at a swift pace until he is safely back in the square. It takes a moment for him to realise that he is still clutching the returned letter between his fingers. He unfolds the paper and reads it. He is a little mystified by the contents but puts it back into the envelope and places it inside his jacket pocket, setting off to cross Oxford Street, and meander back in the direction of Seven Dials, intending to take a leisurely stroll through Mayfair and Soho.

He wonders idly if there is something in all this that he might use to his advantage and resolves to discuss it with Milly, once he has been paid for his peculiar mission. He is so enmeshed in his thoughts that he does not notice he is being followed by a large man in a great-coat who mingles with the passing crowds some ten yards behind him. When he stops outside the Little White Lion, his first port of call, he finds it still closed for the funeral. He stands in the street, pondering whether he should talk to Bilcher for advice or if that might be considered beneath his dignity.

He does not notice the man come up close.

Not until he pulls him into the alley and brings the heavy wooden stick down onto his skull, felling him with one blow.

Harry Shaw lies motionless in the alleyway, conscious of very little in the world around him. He is only sensible of the pain in his skull, and he does not recognise his assailant as the man who interviewed him not half an hour previously. James Aspenn, meanwhile, his face partially concealed by a thick woollen scarf and the collar of his great-coat, rifles frantically through the pockets of Shaw's jacket. His search proves quite futile, and, when he is done, he utters an oath to himself and quietly abandons Shaw to his fate, walking briskly down Little White Lion Street.

He does not stop in his swift progress from Seven Dials until he reaches another narrow passage near by Drury Lane, some half a mile distant, breathless and exhausted, ducking into a small doorway which he guesses to be invisible to the street. He looks down at his stick; there is blood upon it, not much, but blood all the same.

He wipes it clean with his gloves, before he re-emerges onto the road, shoving his hands deep into his coat.

Chapter Sixteen

Stoke Newington to Prusom Yard

I walk back as dusk approaches, following the muddy bank of the New River as far as Lower Street, retracing the steps I must have taken that night, though I can recall very little of it. This time, however, I pause upon a bench on Islington Green, observing the gas men as they clamber up their ladders to light the street lamps, watching the gas as it flickers and flares behind the trees. The evening air is too bitter and clammy to pause for long, however, and so I start walking on, past the turnpike at the Angel, following the City Road against the tide of workers returning home, turning through Shoreditch and along the new road to Whitechapel. It takes an hour or more, but I have already paid my board at Mrs. Flanagan's after all, and I may as well make the most of it.

When I reach Wapping, I suddenly feel cold and hungry; I forget I have not eaten. The kitchen at Prusom Yard is full of heat and chatter as previously, containing the same girls I met before around the fire and one other I do not recognise. Maggie appears to be missing. Dora smiles at me as I enter, but the rest pointedly ignore me and Mrs. Flanagan herself barely acknowledges me, quite engrossed in deciphering the pamphlet she purchased earlier, her jaw wobbling as she whispers words to herself.

I creep upstairs, the girls' laughter resounding even on the landing. It is only when I open the bedroom door that their joke dawns on me: the rhythmic thump of the bed against the floorboards. Maggie lies there stretched out naked, pathetically gasping for breath, her eyes bleary and half-closed. The reek of gin permeates the room, and a fat man in a tatty suit squats between her legs, clasping her buttocks tight as he shoves himself against her groin, grunting with exaggerated effort. He sees me at the door and leers at me, freeing one of his fleshy hands to beckon me in. My stomach turns over, and I spin round and hasten back down the stairs. I can hear them doubling up with laughter in the kitchen below. Mrs. Flanagan sits on her stool in the kitchen, obviously waiting for me, grinning from ear to ear.

'You might have told me.'

She laughs. 'Told you what, darlin'?'

'That she had someone with her!'

'Ain't they just playin' a little game of cards, then, love?' interjects Sally, provoking much laughter from her cronies. 'That's what I thought, anyhow.'

'Cup an' ball, more like!' adds Jane.

There is little I can say in reply.

'I'll be back later.'

'That's fine, dear, you take your time,' says Mrs. Flanagan, chortling. 'Don't forget we expects your board tomorrow.'

'She's as bad as Dor', ain't she?' says one of them.

I leave the house and walk down to the river, the sound of their mockery ringing in my ears. The High Street is just as busy as the previous night, and I am made the same generous offers which I refuse as graciously as possible, though I would rather scream. The wharves themselves are quiet at this time, since most of the men have already begun the night's drinking, and so I wander along the riverside in the shadows and mud, watching the furled sails sway in the moonlight. In the end, I find a quiet space on one of the narrow jetties and sit down, letting the crinoline, now ever so tatty, bulge behind me like a tent: no matter, the poplin is all but ruined from the rain, a waste of good material.

I watch the black river flow around the supports in swirling eddies and my mind wanders back to thoughts of Blackfriars.

And Ellen.

I'm standing on the slope underneath the Monument. It is a bright summer's day, and a man stands beside me, reading the inscription on the base of the column and peering up into the sun. The shape is unclear at first, her skirts and petticoats flapping in the breeze, the unreal quality as she falls. Then the sound of flesh cracking upon stone, the crushed blood and bones against the cobbles.

They added the railings not long after.

~

I wake with a jolt, almost falling into the river. Dora is shaking me by the shoulder and my neck aches from leaning against the struts of the jetty.

'Flora?'

'I'm sorry: you startled me.'

'I didn't mean to.'

'I thought you was going to fall in.'

'Well, thank you for stopping me.'

She smiles thoughtfully. 'You shouldn't worry about *them,* you know: they're like that with all the new ones.'

'No, it's not that.'

She looks puzzled. 'What then?'

'Never mind; let's go back.'

I follow her back to Prusom Yard. It is late, past midnight; all the taverns are shut, and we meet no living thing on the way, except for the donkey that lives in the yard, sleeping fitfully under its cart. Dora tells me that the others are asleep, but she enters the house quite gingerly all the same. She is scared of them, I can tell. Everything is in darkness, and she lights a candle before we go upstairs, squeezing my hand as she leaves me on the landing. In the room, Maggie is unconscious, and the man has long gone; she still stinks of gin, an awful foetid smell of cheap liquor. It's only when I have undressed that I notice her clothes still scattered across the floor. The dress looks new:

perhaps my stolen shilling contributed to it.

It is not long before I gather it up.

—

I leave the room some five minutes later, creeping quietly down the stairs and out to the kitchen. They are, no doubt, used to such comings and goings. Nevertheless, I find Dora has come back down to sit there by herself. Maggie's dress is, perhaps, a little large on me, and Dora covers her mouth when she sees me standing there, carrying the poplin under my arm: it should fetch a few pennies, after all.

'Dora – don't say anything.'

'Ain't that Mag's dress?' she whispers, peering at me in the candlelight.

'She stole my money; it's only fair.'

'Did she?' she asks, though she does not seem surprised. 'She won't be happy.'

'No.'

'Are you comin' back?'

'I don't know. Can we keep this our secret?'

'Won't be very secret when Mags wakes up, will it?'

'Well, until then at least.'

She walks over and kisses me on the cheek. 'Well, she deserves it, don't she?'

Dora opens the door for me, and I creep out into the yard, past the cart and slumbering donkey, running as fast I can manage in the dark, in case Maggie should wake and look for me. I give myself an hour's start then begin to look for a sheltered doorway in the back alleys of Whitechapel. It is a cold night, and, though I have both dresses to keep me warm, I doubt I will sleep.

Tomorrow I will find another pawnbroker for the poplin, but I can hardly return to Mrs. Flanagan's. Even if they would have me back, I cannot pass for a whore.

What then?

I cannot leave it unfinished. I owe Ellen that much; she was my friend, after all.

I will go back to Paradise Row.

INTERLUDE

HOLYWELL STREET TO CECIL COURT

A RAP AT THE door. J. F. Bowles looks up from his book, perturbed.

'Come in.'

Another knock. Bowles shuts the manuscript, placing it back upon the shelf. His eyes throb in their sockets, diminished by the dusty light of the shop, and he rubs them wearily as he bumbles to the door. There is no-one waiting for him outside, merely a gang of street children, chanting his name in unison as they run off into the darkness. He curses them under his breath and returns briefly to the interior of the shop, grabbing his winter coat from a hook beside the door. The thick wool weighs like a suit of armour upon his shoulders but, at least, offers some protection from the cold as he reopens the door and goes outside. He notes with satisfaction that the remainder of Holywell Street, is closing up its shutters, and so he turns his key in the lock, trapping the accumulated wealth of eight decades within. He retrieves a silver watch from his waistcoat and, flipping open the cover, studies the dial as he follows the street in the direction of Covent Garden, snapping the watch back into his pocket.

Bowles's steps are quite brisk, despite his age, and it is not long before he has passed through the precincts of Covent Garden and crossed St. Martin's Lane to reach his destination. The narrow lane of Cecil Court is, likewise, shutting up shop, and it is with some difficulty that he edges his way through the evening bustle of absconding printers, booksellers and shop boys. He finally arrives at a white-washed door, set back slightly from the street, and, composing himself, bangs heavily upon it with the head of his cane, listening for the sound of footsteps within. In the end, a pasty young man puffs to his assistance, swinging the door wide open and beckoning him inside. Together they make their way through the bowels of the house, down to a cellar lit only by the young man's lamp, the floor scattered with sundry crates and boxes.

'The usual package, Mr. Bowles?' asks the man, ferreting inside a nearby container. 'We have some new items what are particularly flash.'

'Indeed? Still, keep to the regular number, if you please.'

The boy shrugs and selects various small books and pieces of paper, bundling them together into a large envelope. 'Will you come and take tea, Mr. B.? We have some brewing.'

'Very well,' replies Bowles grudgingly, following the young gentleman back upstairs into a dingy kitchen.

'Trade progressing well, Sir?' asks the young

gentleman, placing the envelope upon the kitchen table.

'Well enough,' says Bowles, seating himself and making a cursory inspection of the envelope's contents. 'The photographs are all new?'

'Latest artistic representations from Paris, so I'm told, Sir. They'll sell marvellous well with your regular trade.'

Bowles sniffs contemptuously.

'Did you hear about the Ellen Warwick murder, Sir?' says the boy, breaking the silence. 'About the Blackfriars suicide? Another one for your book, eh? It's often the bloody servants you have to watch for, in my experience.'

Bowles looks up at him suspiciously. 'And what do you know about it?'

'Nothing, Sir. Just that it's an interest of yours, the suicides . . . Might we look forward to publishing a monograph on the subject, perhaps?'

Bowles frowns, uncertain whether the young man is mocking him. 'There is a pattern, boy, in everything. The same event happens again and again. I could show you things you would not believe.'

'Yes, Sir,' he says smiling, 'I'll bet. Another time perhaps.'

—

J. F. Bowles leaves the house in Cecil Court some minutes later, clutching his envelope containing the books and papers. He takes the direct route back to Holywell Street and his own front door. Once he has let himself in, he lights a match, throwing some kindling on the fire, warming himself as the coals take up the heat. His hands are still cold, and it takes some time to open the envelope and lay the contents upon the table. He then retrieves a small notebook and, one by one, examines the material, adding a catalogue entry in the book for each item. It is unrewarding work, and the naked limbs, draped this way and that, do not stir him at all. Each piece will find a buyer, though, he is sure of that.

When he is finished with the pictures, he roots under one of the dustier shelves and takes out a large ledger. It is quite difficult to open the volume and unfold the map that is glued into the spine, but he manages it nonetheless. The markings he made around Wapping Basin are slightly faded, and, dipping a pen in the nearby inkstand, he sketches a line north from the river along Ermine Street, then another back down to the Strand, creating a triangle upon the page, imposed upon numerous other lines and jottings. He does not have the opportunity to complete his annotations, however, as he is interrupted by a knock upon the door. He sighs to himself.

'Come in.'

The door opens very slightly.

'Come in will you?' mutters Bowles absent-mindedly, 'and close the blasted door; it is cold enough. What sort of hour do you call this, eh? Not the hour to disturb an old man?'

The door opens.

PART TWO

Chapter Seventeen

Paradise Row

The sound of a door gently closing wakens Hengist Wallace from his sleep. It is early in the morning, and he can hear the rustle of his daughter's petticoats and her hesitant footsteps in the hallway. Turning on his side, he sees that she has already kindled the fire and set his tin bath, basins and carbolic upon the rug. He lowers himself from the bed and walks over to the door, turning the key in the lock before he disrobes. The cotton nightgown falls around his ankles, and his hips groan as he squats down to fill the new chamber pot. It is a strain to then squeeze his aching bones into the empty bath, and, if truth be told, he wonders how much longer he will be able to do such things without the indignity of seeking assistance. Nevertheless, the water is cold enough to numb his limbs, and, with the addition of two further bowls, it forms a chill pool around his waist. He soaps himself methodically, rubbing the stinging flakes under his arms and between his legs, then leans back against the cold metal, closing his eyes.

Melody Wallace sits in front of the mahogany dresser and combs her hair, examining her pallid features in the mirror for signs of ageing. She plaits her long tresses, then twists them into a tight arrangement behind her head, pinning it firmly into place. Her room is quite bare for that of a young woman, principally because she has barely unpacked her suitcase since they entered the house the day before. The splash of her father's bath echoes down the landing, reminding her that she must make him something for breakfast. Perhaps today she will mention the matter of the servant again, since she is convinced they might afford a girl of some description.

She leaves her room, walking softly across the hallway and tapping on his door.

'Breakfast, Papa?'

'Yes, my dear, in the dining room, if you please.'

'Very well.'

She walks down the stairs into the hall. Some of the packing cases still linger by the door, and, instead of taking the back stairs down to the kitchen, she opens the front door and looks out onto the driveway. Their carriage, an elderly barouche, sits there on the path, and Albert, a cherubic young man, crouches beside it, polishing the wheels with minimal determination.

'Albert, will you come inside and help me, please?'

'Yes, Miss,' he replies, willingly abandoning his efforts. 'If you please, Miss, there's a package for the Reverend there, as well. I didn't let 'em ring the bell, in case you was disturbed.'

He nods at the porch where a brown parcel the size of a Christmas hamper sits on the steps, labelled in a gothic script:

Krone's Wet-Plate Collodion Process:
Apparatus and
Manual of Instruction.
FRAGILE.

She frowns as she examines the label.

'Bring that inside then,' she says, 'and for Heaven's sake be careful with it. All the cases in the hall are to go upstairs. I will open them later.'

Albert dutifully follows her indoors and begins to clamber upstairs with the various boxes. His mistress, on the other hand, stands in the hallway and pulls aside the draught curtain that cloaks the entrance to the parlour. She stops there for some minutes, staring at the door.

'Makes the blood run cold, don't it, Miss?'

'It does nothing of the sort, Albert.'

'No, Miss. Beg your pardon.'

'Have you moved everything?'

'Yes, Miss. It's all upstairs.'

'Very well; that's all for now.'

Albert bows and goes back outside. He should not be using the front door at all, but she does not have the heart to chide him. After all, the household is hardly in regular order as it is. Instead, she makes her way down the stairs to the kitchen, puts on an apron and sets about re-lighting the stove; it is the third time it has extinguished itself in as many hours.

Melody appears in the dining room, bearing a tray of porridge and poached eggs, which she lays down carefully in front of her father, already seated at the dining table. In turn, he smiles benignly at her and begins to rummage amongst the oats with his spoon, not unlike a child expecting to find sixpence. Every mouthful he takes is slow and considered, sucking the food between his teeth, chewing it into minute proportions. She is used to him, however, and sits herself down. Finally, he wipes his lips and speaks.

'Did you sleep well, my dear?'

'Tolerably well, thank you.'

'And you have bathed this morning?'

'Yes, Papa.'

'Good. We must prepare for our meeting – can you arrange chairs in the parlour, my dear, whilst I consider the wording of my address? Perhaps the penny copies of the tract on Purity and Abstinence might be available?'

'You wish the first meeting to be in the parlour, Papa?'

'Where else, my dear?'

'Well, after the . . . I'm not sure that . . .'

'Really, child, don't be ridiculous. You are spending far too much time with young Albert. Please do not indulge him in his fancies by adopting them yourself.'

Melody scowls. 'Papa, I would spend far less time with Albert if I had a servant of my own. How can we be taken seriously without even a maid in the house? No-one will come here.'

The old man frowns, adopting an expression

akin to his daughter's. 'Albert is sufficient for our needs, Melody. We need not concern ourselves with domestic trifles. It is society that must attend to our principles and not vice versa.'

He traces a circle in the porridge, as if to illustrate the point.

'Society will not attend to us at all, unless we make ourselves presentable, Papa. Albert cannot dress me, or cook, for that matter.'

'Heaven forfend, child! Such nonsense!'

'It's not nonsense, Papa.'

'Do not contradict me. However, if you insist, I will cogitate further upon the matter this evening. In the meantime, will you be so good as to busy yourself about the house, and do as I tell you?'

Melody frowns but, nonetheless, nods dutifully in agreement.

'Thank you, Papa.'

After the meal is finished and her father has retired upstairs, she clears the table and then returns to the same spot in the hall, hesitantly opening the parlour door. To the best of her knowledge, everything has been left as it was on that night: the reading table, the piano, the painted glass screen around the fireplace. It could be any room in any decent house, all in perfect order and quite respectable. Something, she feels, should announce what happened, some moral stain should linger.

'Where do you think they found her, Miss?'

Albert stands close behind her, making her jump.

'Really, Albert, you should know better than to

spring up out of nowhere,' she says, collecting herself. 'However, now you are here, please see to it that the visitors' chairs are laid out in rows here in the parlour, facing the window. Can you do that?'

'Certainly, Miss. How many do we expect, Miss?'

'As many as the good Lord thinks fit to send us. Just do your best.'

'I always do that, Miss.'

Melody sighs, regretting her harsh tone. 'Yes, indeed, you always do. You're a good man, and I'm sure the Reverend is grateful.'

'There ain't many made like him, Miss.'

'No, you are right there; we should both be grateful.'

The Reverend Hengist Wallace sits in his new study, examining the package delivered that morning, all his attention focused upon it. He unwraps the paper as gleefully as a infant, unfolding the segments of card until the instrument itself is clearly visible. The lens looks clear as crystal, and he peers excitedly into the viewing window, observing the room through the glass. The phials of solution are all intact, and, best of all, the glass plates are unbroken, smothered in multiple layers of cloth. He opens one of the vials and catches the stinging whiff of the ether. All is in good order. Cautiously, though he knows the door is locked, he unlocks a drawer of the bureau and takes out a rather care-worn passe-partout case, decorated in tooled black leather. He folds it open, admiring the velvet lining and gazes at the daguerreotype enclosed within. If only Ellen Warwick were still alive, he thinks to himself. But perhaps Melody will reconsider his suggestion, now that the new equipment has arrived.

After a few minutes' contemplation, he puts the picture away. He must write today's sermon or they will be disappointed.

Chapter Eighteen

Paradise Row

PARADISE ROW.

It is a peculiarly inappropriate name.

I stand outside the house, not far from where I stood after the funeral. It was only yesterday, but already seems so long ago. The round young man I saw yesterday now sits on the steps of the porch, puffing away at a clay pipe with a comical dignity. I open the gates, and he gets up as he sees me, tipping his hat and casually removing the pipe from his lips.

'Good morning, Miss.'

'Good morning,' I reply, adopting my most respectable voice. Maggie's dress has come up quite smart, and I could pass for someone decent, an honest servant at the very least.

'You're a little early for the meeting, Miss.'

'Really? Oh, I am sorry. When should I come back?'

'About half an hour, if you please.'

I bite my lip in feigned concentration. 'Oh dear.

Is there somewhere I could go to wait, do you think?'

'You're not a local, Miss . . . ?'

'Thorne. No, I have just come to London.'

'Well, there's nowhere nearby as I know to be suitable for a young lady. I suppose you might go for a stroll,' says the young man. He beckons me over conspiratorially. 'But would you consider doing me the honour of taking a cup of tea? I don't think the Reverend would object.'

'Well, thank you. I would indeed, Mr. . . .'

'Wiggins, Albert Wiggins,' he says, liberally bestowing a wide grin in my direction. 'I hope you don't think me too forward, Miss?'

I shake my head, and he leads me round to the back of the house. I'm careful to seem tentative in my steps, since I know the place all too well. The kitchen itself seems empty and smells of egg and burnt toast. Albert puts the kettle upon the hob and pulls up a chair for me.

'Well, Mr. Wiggins, this is very nice. Have you worked here long?'

'Not in this house, no. I've been with the family all my life, though, Miss Thorne.'

'Really? Is it a large family?'

'Well, there's only the Reverend and Miss Wallace now, that's his daughter. Have you heard much of the Reverend's work, Miss Thorne?'

I hesitate. 'Well . . .'

'Nothing to be ashamed of, Miss Thorne; he is little known as yet. But you have a natural interest, do you not? You were drawn here and I ain't surprised. He is a great man, very active considering his age, strong-willed. You wait for the meeting, you'll see for yourself. Now, you tell me,' he says, recovering a crumpled document from his pocket, '*Hygienic and Spiritual Purity* – what do you make of that? It has the ring of truth, don't it? It's in sympathy with your ears, ain't it?'

'Indeed.'

Albert smiles at this confirmation of his thoughts and, retrieving the boiling kettle, prepares a pot of tea.

'May I help you?' I ask.

'No, you just sit there Miss Thorne; it's no trouble.'

'Is it the cook's day off?' I ask, looking round the kitchen.

He laughs. 'There's no cook, no maid neither. The Reverend don't believe much in servants. And, between you and me, I don't think they have the ready money.'

'But who does the work?'

'Between you and me, Miss Thorne, I am shamed to say it is Miss Wallace herself. Terrible cruel for a young lady.'

I smile sympathetically. Albert busies himself with the drinks, unaware of the sound of footsteps coming down to the kitchen. I look up and see it is the girl who was distributing leaflets yesterday. She appears at the top of the stairs, still ghostly pale, her cheekbones angular as compasses.

'Good morning,' she says, nodding acknowledgement to me as she turns to Albert. She seems unperturbed by my presence. 'Albert, do we have a guest?'

'Flora Thorne, Ma'am,' I say before Albert can speak, standing and attempting my best curtsey.

'Come to attend the meeting,' adds Albert, helpfully. 'I said the young lady might wait here, Miss.'

'Really? Miss Thorne – I do recall your face from yesterday morning, I believe?'

'Yes, Ma'am. I gave it some thought, and I was curious to know a little more.'

'Well, it does you credit. In fact, we shall be ready shortly – come upstairs to the parlour when you have finished your drink. Albert will show you the way.'

She turns and disappears from view. Albert laughs. 'I said there would be no objection, didn't I?'

I nod and sip the cup of dark tea that Albert has poured for me.

'You were at the funeral yesterday, Miss?' he asks.

'Yes, I saw Miss Warwick sing ... when I visited London once before.'

He does not spot my mistake.

'You know it was in this house they found her?' he says, adopting a confidential tone. 'In that very parlour upstairs?'

He smirks at me, and I can picture the men carrying her away, limp and lifeless.

'I'm sorry, Miss. I don't mean to startle you,' he adds, genuinely concerned. 'It's just my way of being jolly – you won't see anything wrong up there, I promise. In fact,' he says, looking at the kitchen clock, 'you'd better go up or they'll start without you.'

I smile a forced smile, which seems to relieve him of any worries regarding my state of mind, and he leads me up the steps to the hall. Nothing is changed inside the house, which should not surprise me, and yet it feels ghostly. It always did. Perhaps I should not be here, but where else do I begin?

'I'm surprised the house was let so quickly, considering what happened,' I venture, as we climb the steps.

'There's no need to worry, Miss Thorne,' he says, chuckling. 'You won't find anyone hiding in the cupboards. The police went through the place before we moved in, good and proper.'

He misunderstands my interest, but I do not press the point. What did the police find, I wonder? There must have been something left behind, some clue.

I let him take me through to the parlour where a motley collection of wooden chairs lie, in four rows, facing a makeshift podium in front of the window. Miss Wallace is there at the front and beckons me to sit down beside her, although Albert waits by the door. The only other people present are two elderly ladies of genteel appearance, each wearing an unsuitably fashionable and capacious crinoline, and a man whom I recognise as the curate at St. Mary's, having often passed him in the street. Ellen would have laughed to see the room set up like this, like the meanest gaff, although I suspect today's matinee will prove less entertaining.

I do not bother Miss Wallace with conversation, and she seems happy to sit in quiet contemplation.

A man whom I assume to be the Reverend Wallace enters the room from the hall, some five minutes later. He looks frail, with a face elongated and drawn, hardly the vigourous figure promised by Albert. And yet, as he ascends the miniature platform, he seems to straighten up somewhat as he opens his Bible in front of us.

'"*With joy shall ye draw water out of the wells of salvation.*" Thus spoke Our Lord to the prophet Isaiah, and yet, even in our modern times, how many Christian souls can be said to have truly drunk deep from those wells? Truly, we may draw powerful moral suasion from the works of Our Lord Jesus Christ . . .'

—

I remember attending church for the first time, a poky place near to the river, well-suited to funerals. The graveyard is full now, I believe, though they have packed them in three deep.

I wonder where they have put Nat Meadows?

—

The sermon is a long one, wasted upon the meagre crowd of half-a-dozen who are attending to it. Principally, we are treated to a discourse on the necessity of promoting physical cleanliness amongst the poor, but, although the Reverend Wallace is not a bad speaker, I still overhear a snore, snuffling from one of the old women behind us. When he has finished, moreover, I look over my shoulder to see both these elderly persons have somehow contrived to vanish. Only the curate remains, and he is keen to discuss the detail with its author, all but dragging him from the improvised pulpit. Miss Wallace, on the other hand, turns to me, beaming with filial pride.

'Well, Miss Thorne, what can one say?'

'It was very true, Ma'am; it was all very true. I always used to bathe daily myself, regular as clockwork.'

'Used to? No longer?'

'I used to most regularly, Ma'am, until I lost my situation.' I let the words hang in the air before I continue. 'Anyway, thank you, Ma'am. It was most comforting, and I will treasure the Reverend's words.'

I stand up, making a curtsey as if to leave, affecting a tear and a snivel. It is easy enough to do so, if you have had sufficient practice.

'Wait, Miss Thorne; there is no need for that. Sit down and compose yourself. Tell me, how did you lose your position? How were you employed?'

'As maid-of-all-work, Ma'am, nothing more. My mistress was without any family, and, when she passed on, there was nothing for the likes of me. She was good to me, however, and I should not complain.'

'No, indeed. So, you are without employment at the present?'

'Indeed, Ma'am, I have taken lodgings in Whitechapel, and I'm looking for something suitable. In truth,' I add, wiping away my tears, 'I am not sure what I shall do – Whitechapel is strange to me and the people less welcoming than I had hoped.'

'Whitechapel!' she exclaims. 'You are new to London, then?'

'Yes, Ma'am.'

Miss Wallace sits there thoughtfully, then asks me to wait. Her father has finished with the curate, and she walks over to talk to him.

I can hear much of what is being said – it seems I am in luck.

—

The Maid: Shall I dust the bric-a-brac, Ma'am?
Mistress: Not today, Norah. I don't think we can afford it.

That was one of Jenkins's, I think. It always got a laugh.

—

'Well, Miss . . . ah Thorne, my daughter tells me that you are in want of a position?'

'Yes, Sir.'

The old man eyes me up and down like a prize pony. I am surprised he does not check my teeth.

'Well, it so happens that my daughter, or rather I should say the household, is in need of a live-in maid. We can offer the minimum of remuneration . . .'

'I will take it up, Sir, if you will have me.'

'We will require a written character, naturally, and I understand you are accustomed to regular ablution? You will have gathered, I hope,' he says, nodding to the podium, 'that I consider hygienic principles to be of utmost importance?'

'It's a woman's Christian duty, Sir.'

'Excellent – my daughter will show you the servants' room, and Albert will arrange for your luggage . . . you have a trunk or some such, I suppose?'

'Yes, Sir, thank you,' I say, curtseying. 'It will need sending for from Salisbury.'

'Not Whitechapel, Miss Thorne?' enquires Miss Wallace.

I am forgetting myself. Carefully does it.

'No, Ma'am. My mistress lived in Salisbury, and I have hardly anything of value at my lodgings. It isn't quite safe there, you see.'

'Well,' says the old man, 'I see we have rescued you from a den of thieves. Welcome.'

In the parlour, Ellen stares at me with sightless eyes, her body stretched upon the rug.

Now, what would she think of me, playing detective?

Chapter Nineteen

High Holborn to Paradise Row

I agreed to work in the mourning shop not long after Ellen made her offer, that last night at the Eagle. It was not a difficult decision; I had spent many wretched months at needlework, suffering swollen hands and aching joints, and, increasingly, the penny theatres were my one consolation. In truth, I was desperate to escape from the drudgery of the slop-shop. Not only that, but I rather looked forward to keeping her company. Moreover, I must confess, I was still curious to know how she had managed to acquire the place; her silence on that score only served to heighten my curiosity.

As for the shop itself, on my advice the name was promptly changed to 'Warwick's Family Mourning Establishment', dropping the 'Ellen'; we agreed that this might sound more respectable. It was a small musty place on High Holborn, not far from Lincoln's Inn, and, as far as I could make out, Ellen was renting it by the month. By the time I first saw it, she had decorated the windows with black crepe and samples of material, and, inside, a long glass counter had been installed along one wall. There were drawers and cabinets for the silks and satins and, in the centre of the room, a large table and comfortable armchairs for our prospective clients to sit and view their selections. She had even placed a small advertisement in the *Graphic*:

Warwick's Family Mourning Establishment
124 High Holborn, London
Respectfully inform the Public that they are able to supply articles of the latest fashion and best description for Widow and Family Mourning. Millinery, collars, head-dresses and the choicest patterns of the season also available at the shortest notice.

In fact, everything was almost ready; we both thought it was Jay's in miniature. She even had me take some of the material and sew myself a new gown of black silk to the latest pattern, although I noticed she had already treated herself to something a little grander. Once my dress was made, we opened for business.

I must confess it was peculiar seeing Ellen in charge of the place, looking so genteel, but I did not resent being her employee, and I remember standing there behind the counter on the first morning, watching her hover anxiously by the door. No-one appeared for a good while, but, gradually, over a period of hours, they came and investigated the shop. There were earnest matrons and daughters, servants despatched from the more middling households of Bloomsbury, even some of the poorer classes, sad beneficiaries of burial clubs.

Some of them were tearful, most of them calm and composed, choosing between velvets or merinos, examining the texture of the cloth, talking about the funerals as we recorded the requisite measurements. How many days of mourning did we recommend? Would a head-dress be appropriate for a railway journey? When might the gown be ready? It was a decent start for any business. Moreover, I soon found that I enjoyed the work: I had only stuck with needlework through necessity, despite several abortive efforts to follow Ellen's example and find something I might do in the penny gaffs. I knew I would have to do a little sewing in the shop, but it was nothing in comparison with the difficulty of the work to which I had become accustomed. Much of the time, rather, was spent behind the counter, rolling out yards of this or that for approval, trying to look gracious and listen to the customers. Some of them expected bowing and scraping, even at Ellen's prices, but it was no great trouble. In fact, everything went well for the first two or three months.

What went wrong after that? I do not know what was the cause of it: we simply lost our trade. Undoubtedly, some of the customers had come to see Ellen, as much as place an order; perhaps that novelty soon wore off. Equally, I do not think she knew anyone in the undertaking business, nor any doctors, and, consequently, there was no-one bringing trade in our direction. In any case, Ellen herself became dispirited and, to my mind, began to lose interest, leaving me to do much of the work, often disappearing without notice.

In the end, we regularly went a day or more without a single client. I could see which way it was going, but I never anticipated what would happen next.

—

'Envelopes and blotting books?'

It was the end of September, and the shop had been in decline for some weeks. Ellen had gone out for the afternoon and entrusted me with the keys. I had closed up by the time she came back: the black-bordered stationery had been delivered earlier that day. I had assumed it was an error.

'Well? They sell them in Jay's,' she said, as if that was sufficient.

'They have customers in Jay's. How many people did you see in here yesterday?'

'Including you and me?'

'Very droll. What's the point of all this nonsense,' I said, pointing at the envelopes, 'when we can't even sell a yard of silk?'

'I thought it might help,' she said, looking at me like a hurt puppy.

'I doubt it.'

'You don't have to go and flog them in the street, you know.'

She had a way of turning everything into a joke.

'Be serious, Ellie,' I continued. 'You're going to lose this place if it carries on like this.'

'Maybe. You needn't worry. I'll make sure you do all right.'

'I'm not worried about me. Doesn't it matter to you?'

She smiled and took the keys from my hand.

'Maybe I've got something better,' she replied. 'Come with me, and I'll show you.'

She took my shawl for me, turned off the gas and led me out into the street, locking the shop behind her and then calling a hansom from the rank. It was cold that night, and I shivered as she whispered directions to the driver and then got in beside me, swinging the door shut behind her. I marvelled at her extravagance in taking a cab on a whim, but I was intrigued to know what she meant. We set off at a steady trot through the back streets of Clerkenwell before reaching the Angel and heading up Lower Street. When I asked her where we were going, she put a finger to her lips, silently imploring me to say nothing as we jogged along. We reached the leafy square of Newington Green, past the old houses, and went straight up Albion Road. The cab finally stopped as we reached the church of St. Mary's, and she helped me out beside the graveyard, beckoning me to follow her along Paradise Row. The area was new to me then and much smarter than anywhere else I had seen in Islington or the City. There was only one lamp in that part of the road, but it shone brightly outside the gates of an impressive suburban home, a white-washed villa with a short gravel drive, the sort of residence one would normally expect for a banker or merchant.

'What do you think?' she said, teasingly.

'I don't understand.'

'It's mine. I took the keys today.'

'How?'

'I just picked them up. Simple as anything.'

'Ellie!' I exclaimed, both frustrated and amazed. 'I mean, how can you afford it? What's going on?'

I wondered, for a moment, if she was chaffing me, but I could tell from her face that she was quite serious.

'Let's just say I have a guardian angel.'

Chapter Twenty

Little White Lion Street

The noise in Henry Shaw's skull is like a dozen bluebottles banging against an upturned glass. He can taste the blood, flowing treacle-thick down to his crumpled collar, sticking solid around his neck in a brittle black glue, pulling at his skin as he moves. Now he reaches for the floor, or is it the wall? He finds one or the other, his shins dragging on the damp stones, knees scuffed and crawling, raw hands, mud cold and clammy, fingers catching on a fragment of broken glass. He flops on his belly, clutching his arm like a trapped animal, his face gazing on the blue sky, his eyes clouded with tears.

Men walk by and laugh. Then a voice.

'Harry? Lor'! Is that you?'

The room is dark and gloomy with the curtains drawn, lit by a solitary rush light. He recognises the smell of spilt beer and tobacco smoke and a woman's face beside the bed peering at him.

'Milly?' he says, his voice weak and wavering.

'Harry, can you hear me?'

'Milly?'

'How do you feel?'

Shaw cautiously raises a hand to his head, wincing as he touches the improvised bandage of cloths tied around his cranium. His right arm feels stiff and lifeless, and he realises that a splint of wood, half an old floorboard, has been attached to it.

'I thought it were broken,' she says, following his gaze, 'but Bilcher reckons it ain't.'

'Bilcher?'

'Yes, he knows about these things.'

'Bilcher', he says, half choking, 'is a grocer.'

Mrs. Lampton shrugs. 'Do you want some water?'

Shaw nods, finding it difficult enough to speak. Mrs. Lampton disappears and returns with a glass, raising his head and putting it carefully to his lips.

'Drink up. I put a drop of the good stuff in as well.'

Shaw gulps the liquid down avidly, slumping back onto his pillow once it is finished.

'So,' she says, 'this is a fine way to be begging my pardon, finding you half dead in the gutter. I'd half a mind to leave you there.'

He says nothing, closing his eyes to lessen the pain in his forehead. Milly, on the other hand, waves a dirty piece of writing paper under his nose.

'And what's this what Tip found in the street? I know you're awake, Harry, don't pretend with me . . .'

'What?'

'*Dear Sir, I have the letters and the particular item which we discussed. I believe One Hundred Pounds delivered in the usual manner should guarantee the security of these valuables for the future. Please advise the bearer whether you agree to this transaction.*

Yours sincerely, A. W.'

'Is that what it says? I can't remember.'

'Don't play me for a fool, Harry Shaw. What are you mixed up in? Who's this A. W.?'

'Arthur.'

'Arthur Wilkes?' she exclaims. 'I thought you promised me never to go near him nor his bleeding sister again?'

'They must have found it in my pocket.'

'Who, Harry? What's this all about?'

Shaw tries to raise himself a little higher on the bed, shaking his head and pointing to the glass. She goes and brings back another gin and water, finding him squinting at the piece of paper.

'What can Arthur have got hold of?' he mumbles.

'Never mind that. Who did you over?'

'No-one,' he says, trying to sit up and failing to manage it, clutching the bed. Milly Lampton sighs emphatically.

'My eye! You can't even sit up straight. I can't be taking care of you all day, Harry.'

'Don't be like that,' he says, focusing all his effort on speaking clearly. 'I was just delivering a message for Arthur. It was a cash commission, and then, out of the blue, someone bashes me . . .'

'Nearly kills you, more like. Pretty fine message as well, from the looks of it.'

'I didn't know what was in it, well, not at the time. Milly,' he whispers, short of breath, gripping her arm with his good hand, 'Milly, don't be hard.'

'You don't deserve anything from me, Harry Shaw.'

'It was a cash commission, Milly, what Arthur gave me, ten shilling, just for delivering the letter. I didn't see any harm in it –'

'Ten bob?'

'Ten bob,' he says, raising his head and running his hand around her waist, trying in vain to pull her closer. 'Now, no harm in ten bob, is there? Here's an idea, Milly. Will you grant a dying man his last wish, just this once? I swear I'll take no pleasure from it –'

'Where's this money what he gave you then?' she says, grabbing his wrist as his fingers try to burrow under her skirts.

'Well, I was going to see Arthur when –'

She screams, jumping off the bed and pulling down her petticoats. 'I should have known it, Lord knows. Why should I reckon you'd have the money? That would be too much to ask, wouldn't it?'

She screws up her little face in anger and slaps his injured arm as hard as she can. Shaw bites his lip in pain.

'So Arthur Wilkes owes you ten bob, does he?'

Shaw nods.

'Right,' she says, 'well, we'll see about this. Tip!'

The boy appears quickly enough, running in

from the hallway, walking hesitantly over to the bed, looking at Shaw from the corner of his eye.

'Tip, we're going to the Eagle, find my shawl.' She pauses, looking at Shaw. 'It is the Eagle now, ain't it?'

'Milly, don't take the boy . . .'

'So help me, Harry Shaw, he's twice the man you are. Is it the Eagle where he's hiding?'

Shaw nods, helplessly.

'Well, we shall get what's coming to you.' She looks at Shaw, prodding him in the ribs, prompting a loud moan. 'Ten shilling?'

'Ten shilling.'

'Then we'll make it fifteen. Damages and all. Are you ready, my petal?'

Tip affirms that he is and, brandishing his mother's shawl, looks at Shaw.

'How are you feelin', Harry?'

Shaw raises his eyes to the heavens.

'Bloody awful. Milly . . .'

'What?'

'Tell Arthur the man said he weren't having it – the letter, I mean, he wanted an answer.'

'He'll get one,' she says. 'Don't you worry.'

CHAPTER TWENTY-ONE

SHEPHERDESS WALK

THE HAZY WINTER sun shines upon Tip and his mother as they make their way to the Eagle, the same route they used to take to see Ellen Warwick sing. It takes an hour or more, but Milly Lampton barely stops to draw breath. The boy has been to the rotunda and gardens many times before, but this is the first time he has crossed the threshold of the tavern itself, and he treads warily behind his mother. Milly, upon the other hand, merely adjusts her bonnet and tilts herself at the twin doors, arms thrown forward to remove any unwary souls who might interfere with her progress. Once inside, she ploughs through the sea of chairs and half-empty tables to the bar, only pausing to mentally calculate the number of customers and give herself an estimate of the place's daily takings. All things being equal, she decides, fifteen shillings will not be an unreasonable demand.

'Arthur Wilkes please, if you will,' she says, reaching the bar accompanied by her trailing son. The barman looks down at her.

‘I don’t think Mr. Wilkes is accepting visitors.’

‘Ain’t he? Well, tell him it’s about Harry Shaw, and then we’ll see what he accepts. Tell him, if you will, he has a debt needs paying. And,’ she says, wagging her finger pointedly, ‘you tell him it’s urgent.’

The man smirks but, nevertheless, speaks briskly to one of his colleagues behind the bar and traipses upstairs. Milly tuts to herself and turns to her son, scanning the room contemptuously.

‘Well, what do think, my angel? Not a patch on the Lion is it?’

Tip nods. There are a few points where he might disagree, since the Little White Lion perhaps does not have so much in the way of glass or gas-lights, or chairs or tables. An honest man, if truth be told, might even consider the Lion to be pokier and dirtier, with a greater tendency to accumulating tobacco smoke. He knows better, however, than to argue with his mother. Fortunately, the barman returns down the stairs before the conversation might continue.

‘Mr. Wilkes says he can spare a minute or two.’

‘Can he?’ exclaims Mrs. Lampton in mock astonishment. ‘Ain’t that gracious!’

The barman does not acknowledge her sarcasm, but asks them to follow him upstairs, leading them up the same steps that Harry Shaw descended the previous morning, to the very same room where Wilkes bade Shaw goodbye. The Weasel himself sits upon the same stool, engrossed in composition of some letter or other, leaning close over the desk like a schoolboy hiding his work. He swings himself around, however, clutching his coat tails, to greet them.

'Well, well. Milly Lampton as I live and breathe. It is you, ain't it, Milly? Prettier than ever, eh? And can this be your boy?'

'It can be, and it is. Don't play the fool with me, Arthur Wilkes. It might be a couple of year since we last saw you round the Dials, but I remember you right enough. Once a cheap jack, always a cheap jack. We've come for Harry's money, that's all.'

'Now, come, my dear, what's Harry Shaw to you?'

Milly Lampton colours slightly. 'He's a personal acquaintance.'

'Personal acquaintance?' He scowls. 'More fool you, then. I thought a woman like you had more sense, Milly; I really did. What do you see in a man like that?'

'He's educating my boy. And besides . . .'

'Educating?' interrupts Wilkes tetchily. 'What's he teaching him? How to sweep crossings?'

A faint smile plays across Tip's lips. Milly frowns angrily.

'It's ten shillings you owe him and five more for the trouble you've caused, that's all we've come to say. Pay up.'

'Trouble? Why, ain't he coming here in person?'

'You're telling me you ain't heard?'

'I suppose that I am.'

Milly's frown increases. 'He was clobbered black and blue, that's all, delivering your bleeding messages.'

Wilkes stares at her blankly for a moment then, gradually, his paper-thin lips stretch into an ugly smile.

'That's a crying shame, really it is,' he says, sniggering. 'Now why, Milly, should I be paying you anything, unless it's for the privilege of knowing Harry got a good hiding?'

'He said to tell you the gentleman weren't interested,' interjects Tip.

'Really, my boy? So he managed to get an answer then?'

'Sounds like it. And we reckon you owe him for it. Ten shillings and five for the damage. Or else.'

Wilkes laughs. 'Or else what, my lad? You'll have me before the beak?'

'Maybe I will,' says Tip, resolutely.

Wilkes sighs and eases himself down from his chair, silently beckoning the pair of them to follow him. He takes them along the corridor and up the stairs to the room where Shaw spent the previous night. Its solitary occupant still slumbers in her chair amidst the jumble of furniture, apparently oblivious to the presence of anything around her.

'That,' says Wilkes in a angry half-whisper, 'is your precious Harry Shaw at his best, at his finest. Look at her. She can hardly get up. She don't have any wits since he left her. And what did he leave her with? Next to nothing. Robbed her blind. Now, what do I owe him, you tell me?'

'Fifteen bob.'

'You test my patience, Milly, really. He ain't worth your trouble.'

'I'll be the judge of that,' she replies.

'Pay her, Arthur,' interrupts Jemima Shaw, suddenly awake and struggling upright. 'Pay her and let her go. These girls ain't worth keeping on.'

'Don't trouble yourself, Jem. Go back to sleep,' he says gently. Jemima mutters something inaudible and slouches back into the chair.

'You see?' whispers Wilkes, turning back to Milly. 'You see how it is? What kind of man is it, that takes advantage of a woman like that?'

'No, I don't see, not at all. You had an arrangement with Harry, and I'm sticking to it, simple as that.'

Wilkes shakes his head in disbelief, and shouts along the corridor. 'Mr. Simms!'

The large man in question appears like a genie from one of the adjoining rooms.

'Mr. Simms, would you kindly show Mrs. Lampton here and her . . .'

Wilkes pauses in mid-sentence, since he realises Tip Lampton is nowhere to be seen. Milly, equally perturbed by his absence, calls out after her errant offspring, and it takes Wilkes's man several minutes of searching to convince himself that the young man is not hiding somewhere about the premises.

'He must have gone downstairs,' suggests Milly.

'My dear Mrs. Lampton, I don't care if he's gone to the devil. Mr. Simms here will show you out, and I don't give two figs if I don't see you or your boy again. As for Harry Shaw, he can count himself lucky he didn't break his neck. Oh, and do tell him we've changed the locks since his last visit, if you please.'

Milly glares at him. 'You knew all this would

happen when you sent him, didn't you?'

Wilkes lips crimp into a smile.

'Me? I always live in hope.'

Milly Lampton finds her son loitering on the pavement outside the Eagle. She is just tall enough to clip him around the ear.

'And what were you playing at, leaving me alone with that man?' she asks indignantly.

'I was just looking for Harry's money, in case it were lying around.'

'Well, did you find anything?'

'Not right away. I found a loose catch on one of them windows on the landing, though.'

'Loose enough to let a person open it?'

'It is now.'

Milly smiles benignly. 'I see. You're a clever boy, ain't you?'

The boy glows with pride, but, as they walk along, his face darkens.

'What's the matter, my angel?' she enquires, quite concerned, as they cross back over the City Road.

'Was that Harry's missus, that old baggage that were asleep?'

'Well,' says Milly, breathing in, 'that was a long time ago. She's done with him now.'

'Ma, you know Harry?'

'Yes, angel?'

'I don't trust him, that's all.'

'Silly boy,' she replies indulgently, touching his flushed face. 'Harry won't do you no harm.'

Arthur Wilkes sits down beside his sister's sleeping body, stroking her grey hair and whispering to her.

'So, Mr. Aspenn ain't interested. He's just a mite reluctant. No surprise, is it, my dear? I'll have to give things a little stir, won't I? What do you say, Jem?'

Receiving no answer, he gently pats her head and retires to his office. Retrieving a fresh sheet of paper, he dips his pen in the inkstand and commences writing.

Dear Inspector Burton,

I see you are no further with uncovering the secrets of poor Miss Warwick's demise. Might I suggest you talk to the Right Honourable James Aspenn of Manchester Square, who I believe was a close friend of Miss Warwick for some considerable time prior to the tragedy?

Yours,

An interested party.

Once this is done, he takes a fresh sheet of paper and begins a second missive, addressing it to *James Aspenn, 25 Manchester Square.*

Chapter Twenty-Two

Paradise Row

And so, I make myself a servant for the second time in this house.

Ellen must be laughing at me.

—

I light the paraffin lamp and watch the room stretch into slanting shadows that flicker on the ceiling as the flame glows brighter. This was Quill's room, I think, although no trace of him remains. I open the shutters and stare outside, shivering. There is nothing to be seen, except the early morning blackness and the creaking branches of the trees, near enough for me to touch them. Is it four o'clock? Five?

It is far too cold to sleep.

I grab Maggie's dress from the chair and slip it on. Miss Wallace has already told me she will purchase 'something new and proper' for me today. All to the good, since I do not suppose that I will be here long enough to earn my keep. Nevertheless, I already have my duties for the morning: open shutters and curtains downstairs, open windows to air the parlour and dining room, stoke up the range in the kitchen and light the fire in the dining room, lay the dining table for breakfast, carry coal then water upstairs to the bedrooms and, again, light those fires, bathe myself, sundry dustings and sweepings, polishing and blackleading then, perhaps, breakfast for myself before I prepare their meal.

I sit back and close my eyes. I feel exhausted even thinking of it.

—

When will I have the opportunity to look into Ellen's room?

That is the first step.

—

The water proves harder work than the coal, since the latter can be carried in one scuttle per room, whereas the former requires numerous trips to fill the baths. Miss Wallace suggested yesterday that I might leave all these items outside of the Reverend's door, if I felt it improper to be in a gentleman's bedroom. I replied, meekly, that I would never feel troubled to be in the presence of a man of the cloth. This seemed to please her, and we agreed I would light all the fires, regardless of whether she or her father had risen from bed. He is an old man, after all.

As it turns out, the Reverend is asleep when I come to him, and does not even answer my knock as I enter. It takes me some time, however, to kindle the fire, and I hear him stirring and sitting up on the bed behind me.

'Ah . . . Thorne?'

'Yes, Sir.'

'Have you brought the water and such?'

'Yes, Sir.'

He is wearing an untidy cotton nightgown draped uneasily over his withered frame. I turn around to leave.

'Water is the strongest of the elements, did you know that, Thorne?'

'No, Sir,' I reply, hovering by the door.

'Think upon it. Even the mightiest rock is worn away by the sea, is it not? And cannot even the fiercest fire be extinguished by a providential downpour?'

'I couldn't say, Sir.'

He coughs and pauses. 'Well, all except the infernal flames, perhaps.' He peers at me in the semi-darkness, the glow of the fire warming the room. 'My daughter has instructed you upon the necessity of bathing?'

'Yes, Sir. I will do shortly.'

'Very good. The fire is properly lit?'

'Yes, Sir.'

'Then you may go.'

I nod and curtsey, closing the door carefully behind me. I can hear him turn the key in the lock as I cross the corridor to Miss Wallace's room. I knock lightly on the door, and she immediately bids me enter.

'Good morning.'

She is sitting in her chemise on the edge of the bed, reading from a Bible bound in black leather, a golden cross embossed on its cover.

'Good morning,' I reply, heaping the coal into the dormant grate. 'You're up early, Miss?'

'I'm accustomed to it, Flora. Is your room to your liking?'

I tell her that it is, and, once I have lit the fire, I bring in the basins and bath from the hallway.

'Flora, you are sure you will not be missed in Whitechapel?'

'No. Miss, I was paying daily. They will have let the room by now.'

'Then we must send word to Salisbury for your trunk and, indeed, a reference. Your employer wrote nothing for you before she died?'

'No Miss.'

'Then perhaps there is a clergyman or someone else who might vouch for you?'

'Indeed, Miss, there is the Reverend Jones, vicar of St. Joseph's where we attended church.'

Careful, not too much detail.

'Very well, we must write to him today. We will arrange it after breakfast.'

'Very good, Miss.'

She indicates that I may go with a flick of her hand, and so I make my way downstairs. It is still early in the day, and I repair to the kitchen to heat some water to wash myself, although I do not relish the thought of dragging it up to the attic. I find Albert already there, toasting muffins in front of the fire. His room adjoins the kitchen, and I cannot help but suspect, given his impressive bulk, that he makes frequent trips to the larder.

'Morning, Miss Thorne.'

'Really, you must call me Flora now,' I say.

'Well . . . Flora,' he says, plucking a muffin from the fork, 'call me Albert likewise.'

'What will you be doing today?'

'The Reverend will be spreading the word, I think, so I'll be getting the carriage ready. He's thinking of an evening meeting, likely as not.'

'A meeting? And where might that be?'

'Shoreditch maybe, perhaps Bethnal Green.'

'I wish you luck. Will many come, do you think?'

Albert laughs. 'You came here didn't you, Flora? Providence, that's what the Reverend calls it.'

'Maybe that's it.'

I provide them with eggs and porridge for breakfast, as instructed. Once the breakfast things are cleared away, Miss Wallace then insists that we write to Salisbury, to make enquiries of my clergyman and retrieve my belongings. She takes me through to the desk in the drawing room, and I stand beside her as she composes a suitable communication. I decide upon an address readily enough, sufficiently commonplace to confuse matters in the post, and it takes her some minutes for her to find the appropriate words; we spend a good half-hour over it.

The ink is only just drying when the doorbell rings in the hall. The Reverend has already left with Albert, and Miss Wallace looks perturbed; I gather she is not expecting guests. It takes me a minute to recollect my duties.

'Shall I say you are at home, Miss?'

'Yes, Flora, you had better. I will be in the parlour.'

She follows me into the hall, and I give her a decent interval to settle herself on the couch before I finally open the door.

'Good morning,' says a lean-faced old man, standing smiling on the step. 'Are you new?'

Arthur Wilkes.

CHAPTER TWENTY-THREE

BRICK LANE

ARTHUR WILKES. First at the funeral, and now at the house?

Was there something between Ellen and Arthur Wilkes? I cannot believe it.

I have never liked him, I confess, not from the start.

—

I first met Arthur Wilkes when he took management of a little penny gaff on Shoreditch High Street, not much more than a room above an old public house, the Blue Boar. I had spent many hours watching Ellen perform in such places, admiring her steady progress towards the top of the bill, and, foolishly I had resolved to try my own luck. She warned me against it from the start, but I took up his offer of an audition, nervously climbing onto the little stage and singing for him.

'*Single young gentlemen, how do you do? How do you do . . .*'

'Stop!'

His voice, normally a nasal whine, bellowed

through the room like a bassoon. I had expected at least to get to the second chorus.

'Stop?'

'Yes, in the name of all that's holy, Natalie dear, I implore you to stop.'

'Was it that awful?' I asked incredulously.

'Let us merely say you do not have a strong singing voice, and leave it at that.'

'Perhaps in a duo?'

I was clutching at straws.

'No, my dear,' said the old man.

I sighed, utterly dejected, and climbed down from the stage, flopping on to one of the benches. Wilkes looked mildly embarrassed and stared at the empty stage.

'Is there anything else?' I asked in desperation.

'Well, there is one group where I know they are lacking a third female,' said Wilkes. 'You have the prerequisites, I suppose . . .'

'How do you mean?'

'*Jenkins's Allegory Classique.*'

'Jenkins?'

'Ah, I see you have not heard of his new venture.'

I had known Jenkins himself for a couple of months, since he often was on the same bill as Ellen, and was a talkative old soul, if somewhat given to drink. I liked him very much, and the *Allegory Classique* was, I must confess, in its own way, an ingenious idea.

Simply put, there was a problem with the

traditional *pose plastique*, the elegant posturing of young women dressed only in flesh-tone silk, female human statues for the perusal of an audience. It was always an attraction but caused trouble: men became bored and groped at the girls or pulled at their stockings; clergymen, albeit rarely, complained about it, drawing the unwelcome attention of the police or the magistrate. By Jenkins' way of thinking, if one added a story or some patter to the *pose plastique*, one could claim it was *art*; in time, he suggested, one might even charge double for the privilege. Thus, he had set about creating a new act:

Jenkins's Allegory Classique
Ancient Deliberations of Paris – a Living Tableau Vivant

which was to appear fourth on the bill at Shoreditch, as luck would have it, on the very evening of my audition with Wilkes. Of course, no-one would really believe the women were naked, not in poky gaffs where the audience was ten feet away, not unless their eyes were failing them; it was just what they call a *draw*. In fact, the spoken part of the act was to be Jenkins's usual routine, flash songs done as if by a bemused clergyman, not much of the classical about it at all, unless, perhaps, you counted the age of the jokes. Nonetheless, he had convinced Arthur Wilkes of its merits, and was still in want of a 'Minerva'.

In retrospect, however, it was not a wise decision on my part.

As it happened, Ellen was on the same bill that night, though in larger type. I had kept my fledgling career upon the stage a secret, and so she was surprised to see me, wrapped in the thinnest of silk assemblages, hastily tailored to my figure, embarking upon the Shoreditch stage, with two other young women, bearing only an apple to hide my modesty. Jenkins himself was the last to come on, dressed as a comical priest. Unfortunately, before he could say a word, the whole enterprise was swiftly ruined.

I learnt, somewhat later, that the gas-light was a little stronger than expected; the crowd, therefore, had seen a little more than anyone had bargained for, but that was no excuse. In short, the audience turned as rowdy as I had ever seen, roaring encouragement for us to remove our meagre veils and not letting Jenkins speak at all. In particular, Arthur Wilkes, though he was manager of the place, had appointed no Chairman to keep order and kept resolutely to his seat in the stalls; he looked quite dapper in his frock coat and navy blue cravat and, if anything, found our discomfort contributed much to his own amusement. Even his weasel face sagged somewhat, however, when a rough from the crowd bounded onto the stage and made a grab for our legs. At this, pandemonium ensued and, to their credit, several of our fellow *artistes* came out from the wings to push the man back, creating a general knock-about from which few of the men escaped unharmed.

I cannot remember how long the fighting lasted,

but such was the beginning and end of my career upon the stage.

—

I came across Ellen after the police had come and gone and the chaos had subsided; we were both relatively unscathed, though my costume had been reduced to threads in several places, revealing much more than I wished to show. I was looking for my proper clothing, which had been folded away quite neatly before the riot, when I found her and Wilkes engaged in conversation at the rear of the stage.

'Here's a pretty thing,' said the old man, spying me scrabbling around in the debris for my dress. 'Now seeing our Natalie here gives me ideas, I swear it does.'

'Leave her, Arthur, do,' said Ellen, looking at me rather pityingly, as I finally found my shawl and dress under a pile of abandoned props.

'I'm just saying, Ellen, my dear, that –'

She cut him off in mid-sentence. 'One idea's enough for tonight, Arthur. And it's a fine one, so let things lie.'

'What?' I said, pretending to take his lechery in good humour.

'Mr. Wilkes here reckons he will be taking over at the Eagle next month and can find me a regular spot,' said Ellen.

'My dear Miss Warwick,' said Wilkes, 'there ain't no "reckon" about it ... and, if you do me the honour, I will draw up a contract tonight.'

This was unusual: most business in the penny

halls was done on the nod. I learnt later that Wilkes had a particular liking for written contracts.

'Anyway, I really must be going,' he said. 'I need to find our Mr. Jenkins for a few words.'

'Strong words, I hope,' said Ellen.

'I should think so,' he replied, bowing to me. 'I hope to see more of you, Natalie.'

If nothing else, I did not like his sense of humour.

Chapter Twenty-Four

Paradise Row

Arthur Wilkes.

Be calm. He would recognise Nat Meadows, but she is dead.

'New? Yes, Sir, I am. Please come in.'

Wilkes smiles and stumbles inside, watching me with his little eyes. I take his hat and coat and place them on the stand; I guide him into the parlour where Miss Wallace has seated herself upon the *chaise-longue*. Without further prompting, he pulls up a seat by the fire.

'You don't mind me making myself at home, Miss Melody?'

'Not at all, Mr. Wilkes, you are always welcome here. Thorne,' she says, turning her head slightly in my direction, 'perhaps you could find some tea and biscuits?'

'That would be very agreeable,' adds Wilkes, leering at me. I nod my head and leave the room, closing the door behind me. I can barely hear what they are saying, and, although it is tempting to listen, I had best do as directed. It is a good five minutes or more before I can heat the stove to the boil and the same again before I can return to the parlour with the tray, awkwardly balancing the silver and china, then clanking it down on the table. Both of them fall silent as I enter the room, watching me clumsily pour the tea.

'That will do,' says Miss Wallace.

'Thank you, Ma'am,' I reply, leaving the room with a low curtsey.

'She could do well on the stage,' says Wilkes sarcastically as I depart. 'She has such poise.'

Miss Wallace laughs, as politely as she is able.

Again, I hesitate in the hall, but I know they would hear me waiting outside the door. I return to the drawing room and read Miss Wallace's letter once again. It is the same desk where I often found Ellen writing in her diary at the end of the day, totalling up some expense or other, just like she had done when she had her wages to tally from a night's performance in Shoreditch or Whitechapel. I try the drawers, but they are locked; besides, Ellen never used them herself. She had a habit of hiding the book, and anything that was precious or personal to her, in her room; I asked her about it once, and she said it was second nature, from when she stayed in lodgings; indeed, she showed me the place.

Perhaps now is the time to have a look. There may not be a better chance. It is what I have been waiting for, after all.

Fortunately, Ellen's old bedroom, now belonging to Miss Wallace, is near the stairs, and I will hear them if anyone should call for me. Miss Wallace has done virtually nothing to it as yet, apart from bring in her suitcases. Ellen's little hiding place was by the wardrobe, I remember that much. I kneel down and roll the rug up by the far wall, running my hands over the floorboards, testing and prying them with my nails. Eventually, I find one that gives and comes up. It comes free quite easily, and I root around in the cavity, fumbling in the dust.

Nothing.

Why should I be surprised? The police must have everything; I was a fool to think I could find something. So much for that.

I roll back the rug and walk over to the window. The garden is barren and lifeless, the blackened arms of the trees stretch out towards the house. I check the dresser drawers for some hint or token, something she might have left behind.

Nothing.

I return to the landing and bend over the staircase, trying to pick out words from the chatter in the parlour. They are still talking, as far as I can make out. I quickly try the other rooms: there is nothing of interest in the Reverend's room, he keeps it as barren as his daughter's, and the other two are both locked. Ellen never used them either, as I recall.

'Flora!'

Miss Wallace's voice beckons me from the hall, and I rush downstairs, almost tripping myself, doing well not to fall at her feet.

'What were you doing up there?' she asks in mock exasperation, smiling at my breathlessness.

'Nothing, Miss, just cleaning the grates.'

A poor and patent lie, since there is not a spot of dirt on me. She does not seem to notice.

'Mr. Wilkes is leaving,' she says, gesturing to the man himself, doddering into the hall.

I apologise again, retrieving his hat and coat from the stand and helping him put them back on.

'Thank you, young lady. I was just telling your mistress that you would do uncommon well on the stage, with a fine figure like yours.'

'The stage, sir?'

'Certainly.'

'I hope you don't intend to poach my new find, Mr. Wilkes?' says Miss Wallace, jovially enough.

'No, no. Just a remark, my dear Miss Melody, just a remark.' I hold open the door, and he makes his way down the steps. 'Send your father my sincere regards, will you not?'

'I will, rest assured.'

He smiles and doffs his hat, balancing precariously on his stick as he walks towards the gate. I notice there is a hansom waiting for him. Miss Wallace bids me shut the door, and it takes me a moment to register how quickly her features crease into a frown.

'Insolent little man.'

'Is he a friend of your father's, Miss?'

'Of sorts. He is our landlord. Checking on his property.'

I say nothing more on the subject, and Miss Wallace takes me back to finish our letter to the imaginary clergyman. She is so earnest about addressing the envelope that I toy with telling her the truth, that my whole existence is mere make-belief. What would I gain from that, however? Instead, I agree with her that we must go to the Post Office this afternoon and, in the meantime, set about dusting the parlour.

I must be seen to be working, after all.

—

Wilkes owns the house.

Was he keeping Ellen? Was she ashamed to tell me it was him who bought it for her, who set her up in business, is that it?

I cannot believe that. And it explains nothing at all.

Chapter Twenty-Five

Manchester Square

Mr. Aspenn begged to oppose this ridiculous and illiberal measure, calling upon his Right Honourable friends opposite to recognise it as an epitome of the cant and hypocrisy embodied in earlier legislation on this question. He asked whether it was not incumbent upon the legislature to stand firm against deceiving those whom this Bill is intended to benefit, namely females of humble origin, by refusing to elevate the dictate of Law above the fundamentals of moral education. He referred to 13 Vict. Cap LXXVI, An Act to protect Women from Fraudulent Practices for Procuring their Defilement, as typifying the nonsense of legislation in matters where it is impractical to dispense justice.

Bill Withdrawn.

James Aspenn closes his new copy of *Hansard,* pleased to see his name etched once more into the posterity of parliamentary proceedings, almost forgetting Ellen Warwick.

For a few seconds, until he hears the bell ring downstairs.

Daniel Quill walks past the entrance to the square's garden for the third time, pacing in short hurried steps and hugging his arms tight against his chest. His suit is clean and smart as ever, but there is a soreness in his eyes and pallor about his cheeks, and he seems, to passers-by, to be strangely agitated. Eventually, the clouds mimic his mood, and a drizzle of sooty rain begins to blanket the streets. It builds and builds until it falls so heavily that the slate-clad attics melt into the sky and even the brightest white-wash turns damp and grey. Only then does he stop outside his destination and hurry to ring the bell. The footman answers the door, and, with merely a couple of words exchanged between them, he scurries inside. He is led upstairs where he finds James Aspenn sitting in his comfortable armchair. The fire rages, flames stretching high into the chimney, and he breathes deeply as Daniel Quill stands there, hot and flushed beside the hearth.

'Sir.'

'Quill.'

Silence.

'Did Wilkes send you?' asks Aspenn finally, spitting the name out like gristle. 'I won't stand for this blackmail, he must realise that?'

Quill looks surprised at this. 'What on earth do you mean?'

'First he despatches some lackey with a letter,

now he sends you,' he says, leaning forward angrily. 'I haven't changed my mind, you can be sure of that. I warn you, I dealt pretty smartly with the first fellow.'

'I don't know what you mean,' replies Quill. 'I have not spoken to him since I saw you last.'

Aspenn sighs with exasperation. 'Then why have you come here? Why?'

'I want to leave London.'

'A very good plan. I'm most grateful that you informed me of it.'

'Someone is following me, I am sure of it. Perhaps the police, I do not know. If I had but a little money . . .'

'They are following you? Here?'

'No, I don't think so. I waited in the square for some time before I came inside . . . There was no-one.'

'I suppose I should be grateful, should I?' Aspenn asks. 'I suppose I should be grateful that you have called the police here? I do not think so. What do you want from me?'

'As I say, if I had but a small sum of money, to travel, perhaps to Dover –'

'Didn't I pay you enough?'

Quill bites his lip, hanging his head and looking into the fire. 'It is all spent.'

'And from your breath, I would guess it was spent on drink? Anyway, there is no more due to you, rest assured.'

Quill pauses. 'Did you go to the funeral?'

'No,' replies Aspenn.

'Neither did I.'

'Very sensible. They might have lynched you. Hung you by the neck from the nearest tree.'

'I didn't touch her, you know that?'

'I know nothing about it.'

'Don't be ridiculous! You know that I adored her. How dare you even think it?'

'I speak as I please in my own house, *Mr.* Quill, and I will not be contradicted by the likes of you. In fact,' he continues, 'should the police come calling, I will say that you killed her and came running to me like the squealing runt you are.'

'I thought you might consider you owed me something for my discretion,' says Quill, affronted.

'What are you saying? So you intend to hold me to ransom as well? I suppose you at least have the decency to tell me to my face. If they come for me, I'll make damn certain they come for you; be sure of that. Only with you, it will be murder.'

'I don't mean anything of the sort, merely that . . .'

'Merely nothing. I owe you nothing. You were well paid for your expertise, but I have no further need of it. Goodman!' he shouts, addressing the footman who has been waiting in the hall outside. 'See this person out, if you will.'

Quill bows his head but makes his own way from the room, ignoring the attentions of the footman, darting a fierce look at his erstwhile benefactor. As he leaves the house, he does not notice a white envelope which lies upon the floor in the hallway. Goodman, however, picks it up and returns upstairs to his master.

'A letter come for you, Sir, delivered by hand.'

'Well, who delivered it? When?' asks Aspenn, gingerly taking the proferred envelope.

'Couldn't say, Sir. I just found it on the mat as I showed the gentleman out.'

Aspenn dismisses his servant and waits until he has left the room to open the letter. He already recognises the author, from the writing upon the envelope.

My Dear Aspenn,

Further to our previous correspondence, I fear you may not believe me to be in earnest. Rest assured that I am. I therefore enclose a token of my sincerity, a reproduction of the original article, which I am sure will delight you in its faithfulness to the subject.

I look forward to hearing from you at your earliest convenience.

Yours &c.

A. W.

Aspenn tentatively looks at the enclosed piece of card, bearing a slightly blurred photograph upon one side.

Sweat begins to pour down his brow, streaming down his nose and onto his cheeks. He takes a handkerchief from his waistcoat and wipes his forehead until the skin is raw.

—

Ten minutes later, a clarence cab arrives in the

square and parks itself a discreet distance from the abode of James Aspenn, MP. It conveys a ginger-haired gentleman with exceptional whiskers and a rotund man in the uniform of Her Majesty's Police. The latter reads an anonymous note, delivered only an hour before to Bow Street Station House. If he had an opportunity to compare both missives, he would notice the handwriting is identical to that in the letter just received by James Aspenn.

'What do you suggest, Sir?' asks Sergeant Johnson.

'I think', replies Inspector Burton, retrieving the note and looking over it again himself, 'that we wait and see what arises.'

'Not confront him, Sir?'

'With what? An unsigned letter? No, my dear chap, I think we wait and see what he's up to. Maybe someone will pay our Mr. Aspenn a visit – perhaps the very person who scribbled this little gem.'

'A conspiracy then, is that it, do you think?'

'Patience, Johnson, patience.'

Sergeant Johnson shakes his head in deep consternation and reads Wilkes's note again.

Chapter Twenty-Six

Seven Dials

Harry Shaw *swings* his legs from the bed and sits on the edge, propping himself upright with his good arm. Although his feet find his boots quite readily, his fingers are too swollen to tie the laces, and, instead, he manages to loop them around each ankle, just sufficient to keep them in place. Standing upright proves more difficult, since every twitch of his muscles sends a splinter of pain through his ribs, but he is persistent and achieves it. He calls for assistance, but nobody comes, and, with good reason, he assumes he has been abandoned to his suffering. He rests for a few seconds and makes his way tentatively to the door, cursing and walking in slow half-paces like an old man. The stairs down from the landing loom beneath him, each one a challenge to his stamina, and, consequently, he takes them one at a time, resting awkwardly against the wall between each exertion. Bilcher is the first to see him and strolls over, offering his arm in support.

'Mr. Shaw! How is our patient?'

'Not quite on top,' replies Shaw, his words

trailing into a rattling cough, as he spots Milly serving at the bar.

'Come here and sit with me,' continues Bilcher, leading him by the arm to a small unsteady table a good distance from the bar. 'Take a glass of something.'

Shaw ponders, squinting awkwardly at the bar.

'Gin.'

Bilcher smiles in approval and wanders up to the counter. He is forced to wait a good five minutes before he can catch Milly's attention, but, finally, she brings him a half-empty bottle and two glasses, bestowing a pitiless glance on Shaw before returning to her customers. Bilcher, in turn, waddles back to the table, grinning broadly.

'Half-a-bottle on the house. She's a good 'un, ain't she?'

Shaw nods absent-mindedly, snatching the bottle and pouring himself a strong dose of gin before Bilcher can even sit down. He swallows it in three quick gulps then slumps his head backwards, smiling at the ceiling with closed eyes.

'Thirsty?' enquires his companion jovially.

'Have they been back?' he replies, ignoring the question.

'Have who been back?'

'The police ... You said the peelers were looking for me. Don't you remember?'

'I remember, I do,' says Bilcher, patiently. 'No, they haven't.'

Shaw bites his lip and pours himself another gin.

'What have you been up to then, old man?'

'Nothing.'

Bilcher says nothing, but his face suggests he thinks this unlikely.

'Milly went to sort out your Mr. Wilkes, you know,' adds Bilcher, winking pointedly. 'She's a fine woman, ain't she?'

Shaw nods agreement again, rubbing the back of his head and feeling a lump the size of a door knocker.

'Where's the boy?'

'I don't know . . . Out and about.'

'I worry about that boy,' says Shaw, draining his glass again, 'without me to look out for him. Get us another, will you?'

As Harry Shaw expresses these sentiments, Tip is a mile distant standing by the gate of St. Sepulchre's, counting the great stone blocks of Newgate gaol one by one. As he stands there, he imagines the convivial assemblies of convicts contained therein, the cheerful bands of robbers plotting escape and murder, and he would not be at all surprised if they were to suddenly surge forth and break down the gates. If his impressions of prison life are mistaken, if such assemblies are seldom convened within Newgate's labyrinthine innards, he does not wish to know about it. Admittedly, the immense oak doors of the lodge do part on occasion, but only to allow some trifling delivery of persons or goods, and, despite every attempt to peer deep down the darkened corridor that leads within, Tip has no success in his efforts, however hard he strains his neck.

After he has stood there some time, he turns his step westward, wandering back up the hill and then along Fetter Lane and onwards through the traffic of Fleet Street, coming back again to the narrow lane of Holywell Street, which he visited with Shaw but a few days previously. He goes to a different establishment, however:

Hill & Son,
Practical Photographic Artists, Surpassed by None

a place he has passed on several occasions, but not had the confidence to visit. A gentleman with a thick black moustache sits behind a desk inside and watches him as he enters.

'Well? What do you want?'

Tip stops in surprise, since he had expected his intentions to be obvious.

'A photograph,' he replies.

'There's a shop in Clare Market that sells 'em by the dozen, now cut it – you're losing me custom.'

'I want one of me.'

'You want a likeness?' he asks incredulously. 'It's three shilling. Have you ever *seen* three shilling?'

Tip grins and reaches inside his pocket, retrieving three coins and eagerly extends his hand to the man behind the counter. He takes the coins from the boy and views them sceptically, apparently tempted to bite one for authenticity. Nevertheless, glancing out into the street in case this is some peculiar practical joke, he motions the boy into the back of the shop, leading him through a small back room into a yard where a tripod camera is already set up. Another man sits on a stool in front of the camera and behind him is a painted canvas screen displaying a Swiss valley. He stands up as his colleague enters with Tip and smiles as he sees the boy.

'Young 'un, Charlie?'

'He's paid. Do him quick, will you? I'll set him up, and you get the plate ready.'

The other man gets up and disappears into the back room. Charlie turns to Tip. 'On the stool then, lad.'

Tip climbs up onto the stool readily enough and stares into the camera, his dirty jacket in peculiar contrast to the Alpine slopes behind him. Charlie smirks and raises the hood at the back of the device to peer at his subject, then reappears from under the cloth to reposition Tip correctly on the stool.

'Is it finished?' asks Tip.

'We ain't even started, my boy. Tom's still mixing up the paste.'

Tip says nothing, although he does not understand the process. He just stares into the camera and waits. The other man eventually returns bearing a little wooden case and, keeping tight hold of it, plunges his face into the camera and waves.

'Ready, boy? Keep dead still or you'll ruin it.'

Tip sits perfectly still.

—

An hour later Tip Lampton returns home with his

trophy. Harry Shaw is sleeping downstairs, an empty bottle of gin beside him; Tip ignores his mentor and goes directly to his room. There, he loosens the bricks around the fireplace and retrieves his box from its hiding place. His new picture is so small, and it still astonishes him to see it, even though he has seen himself in the mirror downstairs often enough. How peculiar to be captured on paper, he thinks, as he places the photograph inside the box. It is rather in contrast to the rest of his collection: sets of London characters tuppence a dozen, the *Queen and Royal Family*, *Darlings of the London Stage*, faces and bodies he has begged, borrowed or stolen. Then there is Ellen Warwick's picture, the one she gave to him, fresh-faced as ever, just like when his mother used to take him to see her.

That is how he will remember her. She is not dead at all.

CHAPTER TWENTY-SEVEN

STOKE NEWINGTON

ANOTHER DAY JUST like the last.

I promise myself I will not be a servant for much longer.

We did not post the letter yesterday, since it began to rain quite heavily almost as soon as Wilkes had left, and, therefore, Miss Wallace did not care to leave the house, especially as we did not have the carriage. Today, however, the sky is sunlit and clear cold blue, warm enough for me to go out and use the old privy at the rear of the house, rather than the pot. When I return indoors, I find that Albert is already up and about, has got the grill heated up and is helping himself to his breakfast, crunching happily on a burnt muffin. I could swear that he waits for me deliberately.

'Flora,' he says, nodding acknowledgement.

'Albert,' I reply in turn, 'good morning. Tell me, how did you do yesterday?'

'Tolerable,' he replies, smiling and inadvertently spitting crumbs across the kitchen table. 'Thirty or so attending the meeting last night, not a bad lot, if I says so myself.'

I think of all the smallest penny gaffs which must have been open last night, each holding five times that number, but I say nothing. 'I'm pleased. Where did you go?'

'Shoreditch and thereabouts. The curate at St. Leonard's gave us a room for the meeting, which were a blessing.'

I nearly tell him that I know the very place myself. Careful.

'And today?' I enquire.

'Same again, more than likely; handing out the tracts in the morning, meeting in the evening.'

'He must rely on you.'

'I suppose that he does, Flora, but I'm more than grateful to be relied on.'

He smiles to himself but falls silent. I turn to fill some of the pans to heat the water for the baths.

'We had a visitor yesterday,' I add. 'A Mr. Wilkes.'

Albert stops eating. 'Ah yes, an old friend of the Reverend's is Mr. Wilkes.'

'So the Reverend has the house from him on easy terms?' I add, nonchalantly as possible.

'I couldn't say, Flora,' he replies, guardedly. 'They're good pals, though, no doubt about it, used to dine out together quite regular.'

'Really? A peculiar sort of acquaintance for him.'

'I couldn't say,' he says; then, after some reflection, 'the Reverend keeps company with who he likes.'

—

Miss Wallace has little to say for herself when I knock and enter her room. I know she is awake, since I can hear her breathing under the covers, swift and sharp in the cold room. I leave the water on the table and keep quiet as I light the fire, adding the coals daintily, one by one like dull black jewels. She says nothing, and so I leave and close the door behind me.

Across the hall, I find the Reverend is much the same as yesterday, sitting up in bed and waiting for me.

'Good morning, Thorne.'

'Good morning, Sir.'

'Have you washed as yet?'

'Shortly, Sir, shortly.'

'And how are you finding your room?'

'Pleasant, indeed, very pleasant, Sir,' I reply, setting down the jug and aligning the bath in front of the fire.

'We must meet later, Thorne. I desire to expound some principles of the Society to you, so that you may understand our work.'

'Very good, Sir.'

He dismisses me with a nod, and I make my way downstairs again to make breakfast.

It is mid-morning before I see Miss Wallace again, since she does not appear in the dining room, despite my best porridge. Instead, she comes looking for me, finding me making myself busy, polishing the bannisters in the hall. She is dressed in white, as usual, but wearing her walking boots and a cream mantle trimmed with fur.

'We must post your letter today, Flora, must we not?'

'Now, Ma'am?'

I cannot think of any excuse, I must admit.

'Yes – the recreation will do us both good. Do you have a coat?'

'A shawl, Ma'am.'

'Well, that will suffice, I suppose. Go and fetch it.'

I run back to my room and fetch my tatty shawl. Miss Wallace views it with something like dismay and, as we leave the house, reaffirms that she will buy me a fresh outfit.

The weather is still crisp and bright as we walk along Paradise Row. I am not sure whether she expects conversation, and so I keep my own counsel. We do not halt until we come to the side gate of the cemetery where, if I am not mistaken, we both pause slightly in our steps.

'Might we take a walk around the cemetery, Miss?' I suggest. 'I have heard it is quite pretty.'

She considers for a moment but nevertheless concurs, walking with me through the ironwork gates. I suspect she knows what I want to see, and, in truth, she is probably curious herself. We choose the central avenue that leads directly to the chapel, past the ancient cedar that casts odd shadows on the graves. The place is kept perfectly, each plot neatly trimmed and cared for, and therefore it is not hard to see where they have put her, since a little mountain of rain-soaked flowers lies upon the grave and the earth is freshly turned.

A couple of children and their nurse already stand there, looking at the epitaph.

Asleep in Jesus.

Lord. They could have said more than that.

The headstone is very plain, no ornaments or angels, no marble or gilt. I had expected something more. Miss Wallace stands there and closes her eyes, muttering a short prayer to herself, bidding me to listen. I've never understood the value of such things, but she seems to find it uplifting.

'She has gone to a better place, Flora. You ought not to be downcast.'

It does not look better to me, but I hold my tongue.

'You know she used to live in our house?'

'Yes, Miss.'

'Did Albert tell you? I hope he has not been scaring you.'

'No, Miss.'

We stay there in contemplation for a few minutes, and I wonder who paid for the plot. Wilkes perhaps? I do not suppose there is any way in which I can easily find out. Eventually, she beckons me to walk on with her, along by the gloomy pinnacle of the chapel and down the long gravel drive that leads to the gates on the High Street. When we come to the gates, we have to wait our turn, since a hearse is pulling into the courtyard. The procession of coaches, three in all, trots behind it along the path. As we stand there, a tall man pushes past me and strides off towards the chapel, the whiff of gin wafting from his lips along with a half-remembered apology. I know the voice.

Quill.

I almost forget myself and run straight after him.

'Miss?'

'Yes, Flora?'

'I fear I've lost something . . . A ring of my mother's . . . I know it was on my finger when we were by the chapel . . . Might I . . . ?'

'How on earth did you lose it?' she asks rhetorically. 'Very well, go back and look if you must. There is a dressmaker's across the way – I will be asking after an outfit for you, so meet me there and be quick about it.'

I thank her and walk as quickly as possible back through the cemetery to Ellen's grave. There is no sign of him, however.

Just a fresh white rose laid by the stone.

Chapter Twenty-Eight

High Holborn to Paradise Row

Daniel Quill? Another mystery.

The mourning business finally closed for good, and I was not surprised. Ellen made the announcement one evening whilst we were shutting up the shop. She had already been in Paradise Row for three weeks or so, and I had not been there since that first night. In truth, I was a little angry with her, since she had doggedly refused to tell me how she came by the place, keeping it as much a mystery as she had the shop. In the end, I gave up asking: she was always more stubborn than me. If I am honest, I suspected that some man was involved, although I knew of no wealthy admirers.

'I'm sorry, Nat, but I'm closing the shop,' she said, pulling the shutters across the windows.

'I know,' I replied facetiously. 'We do it every night.'

She didn't laugh. 'I mean, dear, for good. I can't even pay the rent on what it's making.'

As I say, I was not surprised, but I was still a

little sad. I had enjoyed the respectability of it, a novelty for both of us.

'Don't take it to heart,' she said. 'It's not your fault.'

I went to extinguish the remaining lamps as she held the door open. Once on the street, she locked the door and stepped back, looking fondly at the sign above.

'Never mind, eh?' she said, smiling.

Ellen accompanied me down Chancery Lane as usual. It was a fog-ridden night, and I still had to walk home or catch an omnibus; the latter was a luxury which I could ill afford. Ellen, on the other hand, normally bade me goodbye when we reached Ludgate, and now regularly hailed a cab, another mystifying token of her new prosperity. Tonight, however, she did not wait for me to leave and, instead, called a passing hackney over to where we stood.

'Come back with me, and I'll cheer you up,' she whispered. 'I could do with the company tonight.'

'Ain't someone expecting you at home?' I asked, rather churlishly.

'It's up to you,' she said, stepping up into the cab. 'I'm not getting on bended knee for you, Nat Meadows.' She said it jovially enough, but I knew she was annoyed with me.

'I'll come,' I replied. 'I'm sorry.'

'That's more like it. I've been thinking, we might even find you some new employment.'

'How's that?'

'Give me a minute, I'm still thinking about it,' she said, banging on the roof and shouting up to the cabman, 'Stoke Newington, Paradise Row if you please.'

'Maid-of-all-work?'

We sat in the parlour of the new house, both conspicuously uncomfortable in such a large room. The place had clearly come furnished and had no stamp of its new mistress upon it.

'What do you say? Good wages, you choose your own hours. I need someone, and we get on, don't we?'

She certainly needed someone to maintain the house; it turned out that any work, from lighting fires to cooking and cleaning, she had been doing for herself. But, of course, it was ridiculous that she should be alone there in the first place. I said as much, but she brushed that aside.

'But a maid? Working in the shop is one thing, Ellie, but skivvying here night and day, even for you . . .'

'Oh no, I didn't mean for you to live in, Nat. I mean, I don't want no-one living on top of me. Not every day neither, not with only me in the house: there'd be no need. No, you could come and go as you please.'

'As I please? What sort of job is that? I don't need charity, Ellie.'

'It's only an offer, sweets, just an idea, that's all. Could be quite jolly.'

I did not take long to give in. In truth, I was worried for her; I was not convinced she was happy with her new arrangements. In fact, I did not think she had been happy for some time.

—

I began my new duties the following day. I soon gathered that Ellen kept to her old theatrical habits and seldom rose before eleven in the morning. I usually anticipated her by arriving at ten or thereabouts. She never wanted me to wake her and, instead, would shout down for me when she was ready to show herself. We often shared a breakfast of some sort and would talk about this and that, any gossip I had from the halls. We were as far from mistress and servant as can be imagined. And yet, for all our so-called friendship, I do not believe she ever truly confided in me. Her evenings, in particular, were a mystery, and she began to talk vaguely of seeing friends and acquaintances, people whom I knew she had not spoken to for months. I knew she was lying and began to think the house was almost her prison. Certainly, most of the rooms were left empty and unused, and she seemed to live there more as a house-guest than anything else. I began to think of spying on her; on a couple of occasions, I even lingered in the evening, outside the house, waiting to see if she had visitors. Then she saw me, and I had to make some excuse about forgetting my purse, or some such nonsense. Neither of us truly fooled the other, I think, and I resigned myself to only appearing at her beck and call.

Still, I never saw anyone else enter the house, not until Quill arrived. It was not more than three weeks after I began my work; I knew it was an unusual day, since the curtains were thrown open in the parlour before my arrival, and, as I walked past the front door, I could hear voices inside. She had not had a single guest in all the time I had spent there. As usual, I let myself in through the kitchen and set about the rudiments of business we had agreed I would do for her; in this case it was collecting up the beetle traps and sweeping the floor. Ellen must have heard me enter, however, since she came downstairs and asked me to accompany her to the parlour. I followed, readily enough, expecting some joke, perhaps some old acquaintance who had paid a surprise visit. Instead, a tall, thin man stood there in a tidy dark suit, greying strands of blond hair sleeked back over his temples.

Ellen made a point of standing between the two of us, hands behind her back.

'Well, Mr. Quill, this is Meadows, our maid-of-all-work. Meadows, let me introduce Mr. Quill, who is to be our new butler, or general *factotum.*'

I confess that I laughed, or at least giggled, waiting for a punchline that did not come. 'Meadows'! The very idea. She had never called me 'Meadows'.

'Mr. Quill', she continued, 'will have the attic room and will let you know if he needs anything.'

I was dumb-struck. I think she expected a response there and then, but I had none to make.

'Very well,' she said, 'that's all for now.'

'Very good, Ma'am,' he replied, turning back into the hall and making his way upstairs, his feet beating out a precise rhythm on the steps.

'Well?' I asked, composing myself, waiting until I knew he was out of earshot. There had to be an explanation.

'Well what?'

'Is this a game, Ellie? Is it all some joke? I don't understand.'

'I'm taking on extra staff, that's all. Nothing to get hot and bothered about, if you don't mind.'

'Staff? For what? What do you need him for? And who's "Meadows" when she's at home?'

'We've got to keep it formal, Nat, for appearances; you know that. If you must know, I reckon I'll be doing a touch more entertaining in the evenings, and I need a man about the place; I can't manage these things all by myself.'

Who on earth was she planning on entertaining?

'And the room comes with the position, does it? Just the two of you alone here? Not much class in that, quite the opposite, I'd say.'

Ellen fell silent, which was often her way of admonishing me.

'Don't you want to work here anymore?' she asked, finally.

'I want to be your friend, Ellie. That's what I've always wanted.'

She looked straight into my eyes.

'Stay, then,' she replied, smiling, 'and do the pair of us a favour.'

—

Of course, I stayed. I even fancied there was a hint of desperation in her appeal for me to remain. I wondered, at first, if she was afraid of Quill, if he had some strange hold over her, but I came to realise that she seemed quite at ease with him. I began to wonder if they were lovers, but then why such a strange deception, for my benefit? As for me, Quill kept his distance; whenever I was there he was almost always upon some errand or doing some job about the house. I could not fathom why he was there; nor was there, to my knowledge, anyone else who visited the place, even after he arrived.

And so it went on, for a good month or more. I appeared when it suited her, cooked her food, cleaned the house, acted the good servant. In other circumstances I might have seen the comical side.

It was more like a farce without an audience.

Chapter Twenty-Nine

Paradise Row

'The natural and bounteous supply of water is God's surest token of his benevolence, my child. And yet this gift is scorned by so many of the lower orders, is it not?'

'It is not to their credit, Sir.'

The Reverend sits in the drawing room in the semi-darkness, sipping the wine I have poured for him.

'No, indeed it is not, Thorne. The purpose of our Society is, stated with simplicity, to spread both the Gospel and the merits of cleanliness amongst the less fortunate members of our society. If only, may I say, the idle poor would pay heed to that great text and concern themselves more with their ablutions, then we would see less of the physical and spiritual pestilence that prostrates them with such regularity. Hmm?'

I suspect that the Reverend has never fought to draw his pail of water from a rusty pipe. I merely nod, however.

'You have a Bible, I suppose?'

'Oh yes, Sir.'

'Isaiah 35:7: *And the parched ground shall become a pool, and the thirsty land springs of water: in the habitation of dragons, where each lay, shall be grass with reeds and rushes.* That is what we seek to achieve, Thorne. Think upon it.'

'I will, Sir.'

He nods in approval. He makes me feel quite uncomfortable.

'Very well, you may retire. I will extinguish the lights. And tomorrow, please be sure to clean the front steps; I saw something of a mark upon them as I came in.'

I thank him and leave the room, heading upstairs to the attic. My room is dull, even with the lamp lit, and I cannot decide whether to light the fire for warmth or simply go to bed. In the end I choose the latter, taking off my dress and wrapping the covers tight around my chest. I lie back on the cold sheets, staring at the slope of the ceiling, thinking until I fall asleep.

All questions and no answers. Perhaps Daniel Quill is the key to everything; he is part of the puzzle at least.

I do not even know where he lives.

Where am I? I know the room. It could be my bedroom or somewhere else entirely. It is lit by a single dying candle, dripping wax upon the dining table. I tap my glass of wine, and it spills in a scarlet tide. Ellen is dining with Quill. She looks down in surprise at the stain on her dress and meets my eyes with an expression between fear and reproach.

I start towards her to wipe up the mess, but someone taps at the window.

—

The noise at the window wakes me. A tap-tap-tap like little fingers against the glass. Half-awake, I open the shutters slightly and realise that it is just the branch of the nearest tree, creaking against the building, like an old man leaning against a wall.

Then another noise. It is the sound of a woman screaming, a muffled voice from downstairs, not cries for help but a sharp screech of anger. For a moment I imagine it to be Ellen, that I have somehow slipped back to that night.

Enough of that.

I throw on my clothes and scrabble about the table for the matches, finally managing to light the lamp. There are no more screams, but I can hear raised voices, not on the landing but coming from within one of the bedrooms. I creep downstairs, holding the lamp ahead of me, like a burning talisman. The noise is from one of the rooms that was locked yesterday when I tried the door, and the voices are unmistakeably those of my employers, father and daughter, in a pitched argument. I extinguish the lamp, since I cannot believe they will have heard me coming, and bend down beside the door, trying to catch something of the exchange between them. The door is too well made for that, however, and the keyhole is covered: all I can discern is a steady sobbing from Miss Wallace. I try and lower my ear closer to the floor, but, suddenly, it springs wide open. I press myself back against the wall.

Miss Wallace stumbles into the hallway through the open door and, though I flatter myself I am rarely shocked, it is hard to maintain my silence. She is half-naked, covered only by a bedsheet clutched to her chest, and, of all things, soaking wet, beads of water dripping down her back, glittering in the light coming from the doorway. Her hair is neatly arranged in a plaited style I've not seen before and, I think, her face is heavily made-up, an excess of powder and rouge if ever I saw it, not mixing too well with her tears. She runs across to her room, weeping, and slams the door behind her. She does not turn and see me but the light emanating from the back room illuminates the whole landing and, if the Reverend emerges, I will be lost.

I hold my breath and wait.

It is not long before I hear him muttering something to himself; he slowly closes the door from within the room, leaving me alone and perplexed.

I should leave it at that, but what do I have to lose, after all?

It only takes a few minutes for me to go back upstairs, re-light the lamp and return to knock politely on the door to the room. I can hear a clinking of some kind, glass bottles perhaps, and, eventually, the Reverend himself appears at the door, opening it slightly. I cannot see inside, but it is very brightly lit, as if numerous lamps have been set burning at once.

'Thorne?' he says in surprise, peering at me through a pair of spectacles. Did he expect his daughter to return? Perhaps he did.

'Oh, Sir, I'm so sorry, I thought I heard something, something terrible . . . There's nothing wrong, is there, Sir?'

'Don't be ridiculous, young woman,' he replies magisterially, though I feel he lacks conviction. 'Tell me, are you given to such nocturnal wanderings? I have to say, this does not bode well for your employment.'

'Oh no, Sir, not as a rule. I thought I heard some kind of shouting – I thought maybe thieves or worse . . .'

'And,' he replies haughtily, 'what would you have done? Beaten them off with your petticoats? I suppose I should be grateful the entire Metropolitan Police Force is not beating down my door?'

I try and look suitably shame-faced.

'If you have any such concerns you should wake Albert, not come disturbing myself or my daughter. You may find I do work here during the night on occasion, as is my wont, but that need not concern you, do you understand? Very well, be off with you. We will talk again in the morning.'

I curtsey and hasten back upstairs, hearing the door close as soon as I am out of his sight.

—

What kind of work is he doing?

Yet another question to add to my list.

Chapter Thirty

Shepherdess Walk to Holywell Street

Eight o'clock in the morning. Arthur Wilkes opens his strongbox and begins to count the money, bundles of notes folded closely together and packed in neat wads. It is a daily ritual, but he could, in fact, already tell you his exact wealth to the nearest pounds, shillings and pence, having devoted his life to the cultivation and cataloguing of these denominations. It is only the sensation of the careworn paper beneath his bony fingers that inclines him to repeat this procedure, day in and day out, in his bleak little office. Likewise, every day, once this personal communion is completed, he unlocks the office door and ambles along the corridor to the junk room, to watch his sister as she sleeps in her chair and to consider her future.

Today, however, he has little time for his usual reflections. He has business to attend to, and, with this in mind, he meets the gargantuan Mr. Simms in the hallway and accompanies him downstairs where a hackney cab is waiting in the road. Once they are inside and the doors pulled firmly shut, the vehicle begins a predetermined route through the City Road traffic, heading towards King's Cross. Their passage is a slow one but steady enough. Turning off through the back streets of Bloomsbury and then Seven Dials, they finally come to a halt on St. Martin's Lane, next to the narrow passage of Cecil Court. Mr. Simms helps his employer out of the vehicle and leads him to a white-washed doorway surrounded by flaking plaster, set back slightly from the main thoroughfare.

A couple of raps on the knocker brings a pasty young man in response who, nervously, bids them to enter. They follow him inside, and he brings them down to the basement, where several rows of unmarked packing crates lie piled up in no obvious order. Wilkes peers into one and roots around, pulling out a book, small enough to fit in his pocket. He flicks through the pages, deliberately not lingering on any single spot long enough to comprehend its meaning. Finally, he sniffs and returns the book to its original resting place.

'Will it sell, Kelp?' enquires Wilkes, addressing himself to the anxious young gentleman who has been watching him closely.

'That item, Mr. W.?' replies the young man. 'Well, it is small enough to fit in one's pocket, Sir, and the text is quite good enough for . . .'

'I didn't enquire after its geometry. Will it sell?'

'Well, don't they alway sell, Mr. W.?' he says, laughing unconvincingly.

'Let me see the latest accounts,' Wilkes responds.

The young man leads them back upstairs to a

room on the ground floor not dissimilar to Wilkes's office at the Eagle, containing only a desk and a set of ledgers stacked upon shelves. He pulls out a single volume and opens it carefully upon the desk, presenting this compendium of profit and loss to his master as if he were laying out all the treasures of the Orient. Wilkes sits down and, without a word, places his finger on the top of the page and slowly pulls it down, line by line, his features impassive as he reads row upon row of figures. Finally, he looks up and, almost imperceptibly, smiles.

'Not bad, Kelp, not bad at all.'

The young man grins foolishly and returns the ledger to its companions. Then he looks thoughtful for a moment and says, 'I was sorry to hear about Miss Warwick, Sir.'

Wilkes blinks but says nothing.

'It's just that', proceeds Kelp, apparently emboldened by his employer's silence, 'I always thought she were a good 'un.'

Wilkes groans, a sound somewhere between mirth and contempt. 'You and many others, my boy. No use crying over spilt milk, is it though?'

The young man looks downcast at this, but Wilkes does not take the matter any further and puts on his gloves, as if to leave.

'Still the same shops,' he continues. 'No-one new?'

Kelp shakes his head. 'Haslitt has closed, I believe, Sir. And I don't know about Bowles, we ain't seen him for a few days. Normally regular as clockwork is Mr. Bowles, buys a book or pictures every day or two.'

'Bowles? That is curious. Perhaps we should pay him a visit, what do you say, Mr. Simms?'

The impressive Mr. Simms says nothing in particuar. Wilkes smiles a thin-lipped smile.

'Well, we must be going. Goodbye for now, Mr. Kelp.'

'Goodbye, Sir. God bless.'

Wilkes and his companion leave the building and find the same cab still waiting for them on St. Martin's Lane. After a brief consultation, the driver heads off directly to Holywell Street. It is still quite early in the day, and, for once, the cab finds it easy enough to manoeuvre between the ramshackle buildings that project over the street and the displays of cheap literature laid out along the pavements. Consequently, they alight directly outside the emporium of J. F. Bowles and once more bid the cabman to wait. There is no gaudy shop-front here, however, just the familiar agglomeration of dusty letters above the door. Indeed, Wilkes pauses for a moment since, like Harry Shaw, he too can remember this place being here from his earliest childhood, a time that now seems like centuries past. He tries the door and gives it a firm push, but it does not open. He tries knocking, but there is no answer and, given the grimy state of the windows, no way of determining whether anyone is inside.

'Not at home, eh, Simms?'

'No, Sir.'

'Well, I do hope the old devil is quite well. Onwards.'

Wilkes lets himself be helped back into the cab. The absence of Mr. Bowles reminds him of his unfinished business with James Aspenn, and he wonders how much longer he should wait for a reply.

He resolves to give it another day.

Chapter Thirty-One

Manchester Square

The bedroom is quiet. Normally, there is some echo of the servants in the hallways or the cook shouting below stairs. Even the coal might crackle in the hearth as it burns. As it is, all the servants have been dismissed and the fires are unlit. Admittedly, the evening twilight still filters through the window, but there is no warmth in that, only feeble shadows that sulk upon the walls.

James Aspenn sits alone in this room and listens to his own heart, drumming in his ears. He has not even washed himself today and wears his clothes from the previous night. After some minutes of sitting perfectly still upon the bed, he gets up and walks slowly to a spot where he can just see the street below. The carriage is still there, however, unmoving and remorseless. He turns away swiftly, as if the very sight itself harms him, and sits down in front of the wash-stand. The bowl is in place and full of water, cold as ice now, though warm enough when the maid brought it this morning. Likewise, the razor and flannel are laid out neatly before the mirror. He stares for some time into the water and then back at the mirror, gingerly touching the stubble on his throat. Eventually, however, he wets the cloth and dabs it against his skin, guiding the blade smoothly along the contours of his chin and neck. When he is finished, he wipes the razor clean and places it on the stand, examining himself once more.

He does not appear satisfied.

The house seems quieter still to James Aspenn. He has re-read some of his speeches in *Hansard* but he cannot concentrate for too long. He takes out the album of his most treasured photographs and reviews them for one last time; each novel pose seems dull and lifeless to him now, and, after a few moments contemplation, he extracts each print, heaps them on the barren fireplace and sets a match to the pile. They burn quickly, charred fragments that dance in the flames, fluttering up into the chimney, then crumbling into the ash. Ellen Warwick is there, and others besides. Mostly they are Ellen.

He watches them burn.

A clock is ticking in the hall, and there is some noise in the kitchen, but he is buried far too deep within himself to hear it. In fact, he has lain upon the bed for nearly three hours and only sits up once, to light a nearby candle, placing it upon one of the twin mahogany dressers that adorn the room.

Again, he looks out into the street but the carriage has not stirred.

He returns to the bed, his stomach clenched and bilious, and crouches down to fumble underneath the iron frame. The photographs are gone; now there is one more thing to be done: his objective is a long bundle wrapped in canvas that he lays out upon the floor, loosening the string that holds it together and pulling out an old shotgun from the covering. This he carefully places to one side, and, unfolding the material until it is flat, he finds a small pouch that has been tucked away, containing powder and shot.

It takes several minutes to load the gun, and his hands tremble as he does so, repeatedly spilling the shot upon the floor. When he is finished, he sits back once more upon the bed, cradling the weapon in his lap then holding it up at various angles, as if examining it for defects. A thought strikes him, however, and he suspends this procedure, reaching inside his jacket and pulling out a sealed envelope, which he lays carefully on the bed beside him. He returns to the gun and, after much consideration of its shape and length, rests it on the floor balanced at a slight angle between his legs, lowering his head against the barrel. It is something of a feat to reach the trigger from this position.

He achieves it, nevertheless.

—

The sounds rebounds through the length of the house. It echoes up and down the wide stairway, from the attic to the scullery. It is a sound rarely heard in Marylebone, and reverberates through the nearby properties and out into the gas-lit square, where Sergeant Johnson reclines in the carriage reading a penny paper. Indeed, he imagines it is thunder until he hears the commotion of residents from the adjoining house.

Inside 25 Manchester Square, James Aspenn lies slumped on his expensive sheets, the silk discoloured with his blood. Even now, before the police can find him, before the door is broken down, before, even, Sergeant Johnson has calmed the inhabitants of the square, even now he has a visitor, a solitary individual who looks at his remains and, if truth be told, smiles as he searches the dead man's clothes.

He retrieves a few objects from the room, and leaves discreetly.

CHAPTER THIRTY-TWO

MANCHESTER SQUARE TO CECIL COURT

'WELL, SERGEANT, WHAT do you make of him?' enquires Inspector Burton, stroking his copious beard.

It is a good while since the Sergeant found the body, and, despite his best efforts, his concentration is flagging. He looks upon the prone corpse laid out across the bed and then back to his superior, hoping for some kind of guidance. When none is forthcoming, he shakes his head very determinedly, as if to dislodge the numerous profound thoughts at play within his mind and reassemble them into a logical construction.

'Suicide, do you think?' continues Burton.

'Oh yes, Sir, by the looks of it. That would be my conclusion.'

'And yet,' says Burton, 'what drove him to it?'

'A guilty conscience, I'd reckon,' concludes the Sergeant, pleased with his reasoning, 'hence our letter from the "Interested Party".'

'Guilty about Miss Warwick? Maybe so. He doesn't mention her,' says Burton.

'No, Sir,' replies the Sergeant, obviously entirely

uncertain of how the deceased might enter into a discussion at this stage in proceedings.

'In the note, Johnson, in the note he left,' adds Burton, exasperated.

'It is curious how they always write a note, is it not, Sir?' replies the Sergeant, trying to recover ground.

'Perhaps. In this case he merely wrote the address of his lawyer.'

'Nothing else?' asks the Sergeant incredulously.

'No.'

'Not helpful, not at all,' says Johnson, again shaking his cranium to no noticeable effect. The Inspector looks at him with an expression suggestive of pity.

'Well, let us continue. Was he alone? Do we know the whereabouts of the servants?'

'They were all given a day's leisure this morning, Sir. We've found 'em all. They says they can all account for themselves, and I didn't see no-one enter the house myself neither.'

'I'll want to speak with them. What state are they in?'

'Well, the women ain't up to much, truth be told, Sir. You might try the footman, a Mr. Goodman; he seems right enough.'

Burton strokes his beard again, playing with the fulsome curls. 'Is he downstairs?'

'Yes, Sir.'

'Well, lead on.'

They leave the room in the care of one of several constables already guarding the door and walk down the stairs to find the servants marshalled in the drawing room. All but Goodman are dismissed, and Burton addresses the footman.

'This is a terrible affair, is it not?' enquires Burton, rhetorically.

'Yes, Sir. Quite.'

'Did Mr. Aspenn appear disturbed this morning, peculiar in any way?'

'A little out-of-sorts perhaps, nothing more. I didn't know he'd do this, Sir, honest to God.'

'No, no, of course not. Had anything happened to unnerve him recently? Any bad news?'

'Not that I know of, Sir, no.'

'Very well. This may seem a peculiar question, but I'll ask you directly, and I expect a plain answer, understood?'

'Yes, Sir,' replies the footman, whether he understands or not.

'Did your master, Mr. Aspenn, have any acquaintance or . . . friendship . . . with Miss Ellen Warwick?'

Goodman looks rather taken aback. 'The murdered woman, the singer?'

'Just so.'

'I shouldn't say so, Sir, not Mr. Aspenn. He's never been familiar with theatrical types, not Mr. Aspenn.'

Burton frowns. 'Very well, is there anything else you wish to tell us? We shall be expecting more from you at the inquest, naturally.'

The footman ponders for a few seconds. 'There was one thing, Sir, it's probably nothing, but there's things missing.'

'Missing? What on earth do you mean?'

'Well, I went upstairs with the Sergeant and had a look around. There's a wallet and a pair of gold cuff-links gone, for a start.'

'Well,' replies Burton, as if explaining matters to a child, 'I expect Mr. Aspenn had disposed of them for some reason.'

'Maybe he had, Sir. They were there this morning when he spoke to me, I know that much.'

Burton raises his eyes to the Heavens, as if about to comment on the untold perplexities and depths of his personal responsibilities. At that moment, however, a uniformed constable jogs breathlessly into the room.

'Begging your pardon, Inspector, but you're needed.'

'Needed?' asks Burton, annoyed by the interruption. 'What is it now?'

'It's a murder Sir, unpleasant by all accounts. No-one else on duty at Bow Street.'

'Nice to be kept busy, ain't it Sir?' grins Johnson.

—

The door to Bowles's shop has been broken down, and, by the time Burton arrives, even though it is close to midnight, a small crowd is gathered round the darkened doorway on Holywell Street, held back by two police constables. Both these men recognise the Inspector, however, and they assist as he pushes his way through the spectators to the musty interior where a sergeant stands guard over the shop. The latter nods acknowledgement of his superior and obligingly shines his bull's eye over the debris, revealing how every shelf and its accompanying pile of books has been flung down to the ground, creating a vast fallen mountain of paper in the centre of the room. The slightest movement of the two men kicks up choking showers of dust and so, for a moment, they both stand perfectly still, catching their breath and gazing at the mess. Both notice the sickly scent of rotten meat.

'It's Bowles, the owner, Sir,' says one of the men, watching Burton as he surveys the scene.

'Upstairs?' asks the Inspector, seeing no trace of the body.

'Sorry, Sir, he's under here,' elaborates the man, shifting a couple of substantial volumes to reveal a bruised human hand poking through the accumulated paper. 'We thought he'd been crushed, accidental like, at first, but then we saw his stomach.'

'Stomach?'

'Stabbed, Sir, large wound with a sharp knife. Quite ripe, ain't he, Sir? Been here a few days, I'd say.'

'Who found him?'

'Shop next door noticed the smell, Sir. We had to break in.'

'The door was locked?'

'Oh yes. They probably got out the back.'

Burton peels back a handsome atlas to look at the body. The flesh is encrusted with blood, but, nevertheless, the wide sweep of the blade is visible enough, just below the rib cage. It reminds him of another corpse, a similar wound, and it takes a moment for his mind to make the connection.

Ellen Warwick.

Interlude

Fleet Street to Abney Park

Daniel Quill stands outside his old studio upon the corner of Whitefriars and Fleet Street; the windows are covered with boards and the name

Daniel Quill,
Photographic Portraits

is barely visible, the black paint smothered in dirt and dust from the passing traffic. It is some months since he left the place, but it has not yet been let.

He takes another swig from the gin in his flask, looking down once more at the newspaper he bought this morning.

Tragic Death of James Aspenn, MP.

Nothing has gone right since he met James Aspenn.

'Mr. Quill?'

'Indeed, Sir. What may I do for you?'

'I have been admiring your artistry. The specimens in your window are all your own work?'

'On my honour, Sir.'

'You use the latest ambrotype process, I see.'

'Indeed, Sir. You know something of our business?'

'I dabble. Tell me, do you have any, how shall I say, artistic studies?'

'How do you mean?'

'Come now, no need to be coy. A mutual friend Mr. Wilkes recommended you most strongly.'

'Ah. Well, I keep the stronger material to one side. Would you care to have a look?'

'Ah, now this is excellent. The girls are known to you?'

'Nothing like that, Sir. I just pay them by the hour.'

'Tell me, in general terms, you do a brisk trade?'

'I do tolerably well, Sir.'

'Well, perhaps you might do better. I wonder, would you consider taking on a commission for me? I would reward you handsomely.'

'I fear you misjudge me, Sir. I do not procure women – the pictures are artistic, as you say.'

'Be calm, Mr. Quill. I admire your discretion. I have a lady in mind, that much is settled. Perhaps you might call on me tomorrow morning, and we can discuss this further. Here is my card . . .'

James Aspenn
25 Manchester Square
Marylebone

An hour later, Daniel Quill partakes once more from the cheap spirits in his flask, then turns the corner into Manchester Square. The police are there, of course, a pair of blue-uniformed constables guarding the front door, whilst a few curious strangers mill about outside and talk amongst themselves.

He notices a figure, idling by the railings, also watching the house. It takes him a moment to recognise the face.

He does not give it a thought. He turns and runs.

PART THREE

Chapter Thirty-Three

Paradise Row to Scotland Yard

It is the same dream, each time without fail.

I come upon Blackfriars Bridge from the Southwark shore for the first time. There is no gaslight, not as yet; there is only the waning moon flitting between the clouds, like the crescent blade of a sickle swung up high; it glints for an instant above Ludgate's rooftops, threatening to crop the smoking columns that poke above the city slates; it slips away and everything becomes cloud and smoke.

There is a toll for crossing the bridge, levied by an old man in the gatehouse. He looks at me as if he suspects my purpose, and, indeed, it is not hard to guess. If that is the case, he takes my money readily enough and lets me walk on. The stonework itself has just been finished, and the wooden scaffold still projects from beneath the arches; it cannot stop me from falling.

The river engulfs me, cold and black, and I think to myself, 'I have cheated death.'

Awake again.

The Reverend is not awake when I bring him his bath. I had expected him to chastise me about last night, but he merely snores in his bed, oblivious to my presence. Miss Wallace, upon the other hand, is awake but noticeably subdued and, complaining of a chill, says that she will remain in her room for most of the day. She looks thinner and weaker than ever; I bring her some onion soup for lunch, but she barely touches it. The Reverend, meanwhile, rises at nine o'clock and secludes himself in the drawing room downstairs; he seems in quite high spirits. When I am certain that neither of them is nearby, I try the door to the back bedroom, but, as I had expected, it has been locked once more.

Neither father nor daughter chooses to leave the house all day, and, since the kitchen is fully stocked, I remain indoors myself and try to appear busy, occasionally colliding with Albert below stairs as he makes his regular invasions of the larder. In truth, I spend much of my time searching the house for some trace of Ellen, an exercise which proves quite futile. My only consolation is that there is still no response to Miss Wallace's letter enquiring after my character; no doubt the Post Office is making sincere efforts to locate my imaginary clergyman, but it will be another day or two before it is returned.

I am thinking of this when, as I light the lamps before dinner, the Reverend beckons me into the drawing room. For a moment, I fear he has found me out. Fortunately, it is another matter entirely.

'Thorne, I hope I was not too harsh with you last night?'

'Oh no, Sir.'

'It is unfortunate that you found me at a critical moment, but, as the Lord knows, it is beholden upon us not to be quick to anger.'

'I hope you can forgive me, Sir.'

'That is my Christian duty, young woman. Now, let us discuss more pleasant matters. We have not set your leisure day this month?'

'No, Sir.'

'Well, then let us say tomorrow. Have it done with, so we know where we stand.'

'Thursday, Sir?'

'I realise a Sunday would be more usual, but we have a greater need of you upon the Sabbath. You will be attending our service, after all, and so lose nothing by it.'

'Thank you, Sir.'

'Very well, you may go. Naturally, you will prepare breakfast, and we shall expect you back by dusk.'

I curtsey and leave. It seems I shall not get an evening of my own, although I suppose that is not unusual.

I know what I shall do.

Tomorrow, I will talk to the police.

—

How did it go, another one of Jenkins's?

Q: What's the worst ailment afflictin' the poor?

A: A touch of the blue collarer.
Not one of his best, I grant you.

—

Thursday.

The outfit Miss Wallace ordered for me arrives, delivered first thing. It is not just the frock and apron but also fresh stockings and a flannel petticoat. She has even provided a new woollen shawl; no doubt she is ashamed of my old one. Once breakfast is done, I try it all on, at her insistence.

'It is a good fit, is it not?' she says, looking me over.

'Yes, Miss, excellent.'

'Be careful not to dirty it too much, if you will. I understand my father has given you a day's leisure?'

'Yes, Miss.'

'What shall you do with it? Do you have any plans?'

'I thought I might go into town and see the sights, if there's no objection, Miss.'

'Oh dear. I hope you will not wander too far, Flora. There are so many insalubrious places, even in the best parts of London. Do you know the way?'

'Yes, I think so, thank you Miss.'

—

It takes two hours or more to reach Whitehall; I do not have a fare for the omnibus, and so I walk, down to the Angel, then on through Pentonville and Bloomsbury, then down St. Martin's Lane. Once I am there, I discover that I cannot locate Scotland Yard; it is one of the few corners of the city that has escaped me in the past. Finally, I am forced to buttonhole a regular constable who directs me grudgingly to the buildings, which are meaner and more dilapidated than I might have expected. I am grateful, however, for my smart new costume, since even in this outfit the man hardly deigns to talk to me. What would he have made of me before, I wonder? The clerk to whom he directs me is little better, peering down at me from behind a raised desk in his dingy hallway.

'You do realise this ain't a regular Station House, don't you, Miss?'

'I must speak to someone about Ellen Warwick, the woman who was murdered.'

The clerk chuckles. 'Oh, the one what was murdered? Well, that's a different matter. Different matter entirely, Miss.'

'Yes,' I persist. 'I'm her sister.'

That stops him. I am a convincing liar, even if I say so myself. Ellen was an orphan, I believe; she knew no more about her family than I do.

'Come on now, Miss,' he says, laughing more hesitantly. 'We ain't got time for games here. Miss Warwick didn't have no sister, did she now?'

It is never wise to rely on tears in these circumstances, especially if there are other women present, but in this case I make an exception. I even have a very becoming new handkerchief, supplied with Miss Wallace's outfit, in which to hide my face. The man visibly wilts.

'Come on, now, Miss, no need for that . . .'

'It's true,' I snivel. 'I am her sister . . . we were separated in the workhouse when they sent us into service . . .'

I can feel the little drama writing itself.

'Well, I don't know, Miss. I mean . . .'

'Is there no-one I can speak to?' I ask, looking up at him with dewy eyes.

The man blushes. 'Well, perhaps I can find someone.'

'Please, I would be so grateful.'

'Wait there.'

I sit down upon the bench provided and watch the clerk disappear into a nearby office. He returns in a few minutes but bids me to wait once more, whilst he retrieves a set of keys from a cabinet behind his desk. Finally, I am taken to a dim little room on the first floor of Scotland Yard, empty but for a plain wooden table and pair of chairs.

'Wait here, please, Miss,' he says again, leaving and closing the door behind him.

—

I wait for at least two hours. A church bell rings one o'clock before the door finally opens and a well-rounded fellow, dressed in a Sergeant's uniform, enters the room and greets me.

'Now, Miss . . .'

'Warwick. Sarah Warwick.'

'Ah yes, Miss Warwick. My name is Johnson, Sergeant Johnson. You have something to tell us?'

'I'd hoped,' I say with a quaking voice, 'you might tell me who killed my sister.'

'Ah, well Miss. That's a confidential police matter.'

I can tell from the look of him that clearly they have little idea. I try the tears again, but not so extravagantly this time. He looks suitably discomfitted.

'No need to distress yourself, Miss. Come now. It's very natural, I'm sure. It's just,' he says, trying to find the correct words, 'well, with all due respect, Miss, Miss Warwick weren't known to have a sister.'

'Why would I lie about such a thing?' I ask, wiping my cheeks.

'Well now, I never said that, did I, Miss? It's just the facts we require, plain and simple. The Metropolitan Police Force must be sure of the facts, Miss, otherwise we aren't worthy of the name, you see. Do you have anything pertaining to the facts, some proof of the matter?'

I look thoughtful for a suitable juncture and shake my head. The Sergeant frowns.

'Unless,' I add tentatively, 'Ellen's diary – she always kept a diary, a little notebook . . . that might help? Perhaps she may have written something of me.'

'Oh no, Miss,' says Johnson, eyeing me with renewed suspicion. 'There weren't no diary, not in this case.'

'Are you sure?'

The Sergeant looks offended. 'I think we would know if there was, Miss, don't you? Now, tell me more about when you last saw your sister . . .'

It takes a good hour to extricate myself from Sergeant Johnson. I have to be careful. I spin a story about two sisters, separated in the workhouse; it is not implausible in itself, but I invent more names and addresses than I care to remember. By the time he has checked any of the details, he will not find me again. And I have done nothing wrong, after all.

I leave Whitehall as swiftly as possible and wander back towards Islington, through the evening crowds. I had thought that I might look at the diary, that there might be something whose significance only I would understand.

So much for that. But where next?

Chapter Thirty-Four

Abney Park

Daniel Quill *sits* upon the bench, clutching his empty bottle. He lets his head fall forward and stares at Ellen's photograph, the albumen print which he made for himself.

'A little more to the left, raise your shoulder.'

'Really, Mr. Quill, you're very demanding, ain't you?'

'That is my job.'

'You ain't the one freezin' to death.'

'Please, Miss Warwick, I beg you, just a little more on your side, as in the lithograph I showed you.'

'Miss? Ain't you polite, all things considered?'

'I'm releasing the shutter. Be still, if you please.'

'Call me Ellie.'

'Very well . . . Ellie. Please be still.'

Daniel Quill wakes, his mouth dry and his head spinning; above him is a dark blue winter sky.

He roots in his pocket for another bottle, but it also comes out empty, just like the one beside him. He slumps back, knowing he is dissatisfied but unable to recall why.

'How do they look? Are they quality?'

'Mr. Aspenn will be very gratified, I am sure.'

'And you, Mr. Quill? Do they gratify you?'

'Ellie, please. He will hear you.'

'No, he's getting dressed.'

'All the same. I am tired of playing games.'

'Tell him, then, if you like. Tell him you love me. See what he says.'

'Maybe I will. We could just leave, you realise that?'

'I don't think so.'

Now he is lying upon his bed in Paradise Row.

He gets up. Around him are broken negatives, fragments of blackened glass; each one has blurred flesh, arms and legs trailing in ghostly sweeps across the plates. The camera itself has been broken, the lens deliberately shattered, the shutter torn out.

Nothing with her face, though. Why does he have nothing with her face?

He walks downstairs. She lies there upon the floor. Her eyes are quite empty of life, but he feels that someone is watching him.

He runs back upstairs and begins to gather up the photographs.

A different time. The rosy glow of her skin lit by candles.

She calls him 'Daniel' now and touches his hand.

The shutter slides shut.

Chapter Thirty-Five

Seven Dials

Inspector Burton and Sergeant Johnson walk leisurely along Monmouth Street. No-one looks them in the eye. Not the second-hand clothes men, nor the cobblers banging nails into half-finished boots, nor the grubby children who play in the gutter. But, nonetheless, they do not go unnoticed, and the word 'police' is passed from tenant to tenant, whispered between tenement walls, sliding down rooftops, running along the street, until even the stones in St. Giles' churchyard chatter anxiously amongst themselves. Harry Shaw, however, having over-indulged himself the previous evening, has hardly spoken to a soul since he awoke. Consequently, he is the only man in Seven Dials surprised to see the pair of policemen enter the Little White Lion, where he lies slumped by the bar.

'Good morning, Harry. Don't stand up on our account,' intones Burton as they amble towards him.

Shaw raises his head, half-asleep but recognising his own name.

'You do recognise me, don't you, Harry?' asks Burton, looking at the dazed and dishevelled man in front of him.

'Inspector Burton, I hope I finds you well,' mutters Shaw, raising his head.

'Better than yourself, I'll warrant. I don't see you as a brawler, Harry,' says Burton, looking at the marks upon his face. 'Did someone take an exception to you?'

'Something like that.'

'Well, we were looking for you, you know, a day or two ago. It was going to be a simple matter of identifying a body, but it's getting a bit late for that now.'

'They don't keep, see?' interjects Johnson, helpfully.

'The Sergeant is correct. A body does not keep. And, as it happens, events have overtaken us.'

'My dear Inspector, I've been here for three full days, haven't moved from this house. Ask anyone.'

'Ask anyone?' Burton laughs, rubbing his beard. 'That's a jolly good one, isn't it, Sergeant? Ask anyone indeed! They'll all vouch for you, will they, the honest citizens that frequent this little tea-room? Talking of which, where is the good Mrs. Lampton?'

'Out.'

'Good, then we won't be disturbing her. Johnson, search upstairs; I'll look down here.'

Shaw groans and sinks down onto the table as Johnson advances up the stairs. Burton, meanwhile, prowls around the room.

'Now, my man, let us consider your situation. It doesn't look too good for you.'

Shaw looks up at him, perplexed. 'What doesn't?'

Burton smiles and retrieves a notebook from his jacket. 'Do you know what my business is?'

Shaw shrugs, tactful enough to keep silent.

'To be blunt, Harry, it is suicides and murders, plain and simple. And, when we have more than one such incident all mixed up together, do you know what Her Majesty's Police look for?'

'The body?'

'Watch your lip. We look for the connection. And you, my dear Mr. Shaw, you are the connection.'

Shaw laughs. 'You're pulling my leg, ain't you?'

Burton shakes his head solemnly. 'I was surprised, to tell you the truth, Harry, but let us examine some facts: Natalie Meadows, drowned, thought to be a suicide. You were there, were you not?'

'You were at the damned inquest,' says Shaw, annoyed. 'You know I was. What are you saying?'

'Well,' says Burton, reading calmly from his notebook, 'let us turn to John Bowles of Holywell Street, found murdered last night.'

'Dead? Bowles?'

'Dead. You were seen entering his premises, together with a boy, four days ago. His neighbour saw you talking to him. Never saw no-one else go in after that.'

'Well, that settles it, don't it? I must have bleedin' talked him to death,' replies Shaw sarcastically, even though his face betrays his concern.

'Well, shall we discuss the Right Honourable James Aspenn? A "Mr. Shaw" called at his house three days ago, according to the servants. He looked very much like you, as far as I can make out. Do you deny it? '

'What of it?'

'He's dead, another suicide, by the look of it, at least. Quite possibly theft as well. An odd person for you to be calling upon?'

'Well, it ain't nothing to do with me.'

'And we would like to make a few enquiries pertaining to Miss Ellen Warwick, as well.'

'Her as well? Well, bring them all on, the more the bleeding merrier!'

'Less of that, Harry. This is a serious matter. We need to have a long talk with you down the Yard.'

'You are joking?'

Burton smiles and shakes his head. In the meantime there is the sound of a scuffle on the stairs and Johnson descends, dragging Tip Lampton behind him by the collar. 'No valuables up there, Sir, nothing except the boy.'

'Hmm. That's Milly's lad, ain't it? Was this the boy you took to see Bowles?' asks Burton.

'No,' mutters Shaw, not particularly convincingly.

'Very well, if that's how you want it. I suggest you both come with us. Sergeant – we'll go to St. Giles's Station House, I think. That is nearest.'

'Very good, Sir.'

The Sergeant bustles Tip towards the door,

ignoring his protests; Shaw follows with Burton. He is in no fit state to argue the matter and cannot stop thinking of what Milly will say when she returns and finds the place empty. Outside, however, the street seems unusually busy, and, as they leave the pub, a crowd of local inhabitants mills around them. There are fifty or more, a shabby gathering of men, women and children from the far corners of the Dials; it is obvious they are waiting with a purpose. Burton steps forward with Shaw but a couple of the men jostle him and push them back onto the doorstep.

'What they done?' shouts a voice from the back.

'They must answer questions pertaining to a murder,' says Burton with as much majesty as he can muster. 'Stand aside.'

'Harry ain't killed no-one,' shouts another voice. Shaw recognises it as Bilcher, blessing him under his breath.

'There are questions to answer, that is all – stand aside, I say,' shouts Burton, pushing forward into the crowd with the Sergeant following behind.

'They ain't done nothin',' shouts one voice, then another.

Nevertheless, the crowd parts to let them through, and they make some headway through the narrow corridor, flanked on both sides by surly men and red-faced women. For a moment, it appears that the policemen may escape unharmed until, as if at some silent signal, hands begin to reach out, tugging their clothes, hob-nailed boots kicking at their legs. They try to press on, but it does not take much for Tip Lampton to wriggle free and slip into the tangle of bodies. A few moments later, though he is not half so nimble, Shaw does likewise, pulled out of the scrum by the admirable Bilcher. Once they are free, a cry goes up and a hail of pummelling blows descend upon Her Majesty's Police, a barrage of boots, fists and elbows. To their credit, the policemen defend themselves quite admirably, and, since it is too early in the day for strong drink to have taken hold, they are merely punched, kicked and spat upon as the mob sweeps them along. In the end, despite their breathless threats of dire consequences, they are forced to run, limping and bruised, in the direction of St. Martin's.

'Well,' says Bilcher, surveying the jeering crowd, 'what have you been up to, Mr. Shaw?'

Shaw leans breathlessly against a doorway. 'Milly will kill me.'

Bilcher chuckles, lending him support as he staggers back inside the Little White Lion. 'Perhaps you should give yourself up.'

Chapter Thirty-Six

Seven Dials

'You'll drag us down with you, or I'm a Dutchman. I knew it. I've always knowed it. And now I know I'm right.'

Milly Lampton sits on a chair in Bilcher's attic, anxiously looking at the empty street below through the small window. It is an hour or more since the departure of Messrs. Burton and Johnson, and the unruly crowd has long since dispersed, knowing better than to wait for the police to come back. Standing up, Milly paces around the room like an animated doll, her face wrinkled in displeasure, deliberately avoiding Shaw's gaze.

'Milly, please,' begs Shaw, nursing a cloudy glass containing brandy. 'I ain't even done anything. It was you that said I should see Bowles in the first place.'

'So you're blaming me, are you? I didn't tell you to murder no-one, did I!'

'I didn't touch him, I swear!' exclaims Shaw, slamming his drink down on the table such that half of it spills out onto the floor.

'It don't matter what you did, Harry Shaw, if you ain't noticed. It's what they think that matters, and they even thinks my angel had something to do with it.'

Tip sits in the corner, looking dispirited. He has watched his mother raging at Harry Shaw for several minutes, and he is growing tired of it.

'And they'll come back,' adds Bilcher, helpfully, 'the Peelers.'

'Yes,' agrees Milly, 'he's right; the Peelers will come back by the dozen and they won't take no for an answer this time, will they? Well, you can't stop at the Lion no more, that's for certain, neither of you.'

It is hard to tell whether Tip or Shaw is the more aggrieved.

'They can stay up here a little while, Milly,' offers Bilcher, 'if you like.'

'Well, at least someone has their heads screwed on straight – done,' she replies, bestowing a smile upon Bilcher.

'Don't I have a say?' mutters Shaw.

'It strikes me you don't, Harry, unless you have a better idea. Anyhow, that'll do for now. I best go and open up, though Lord knows if anyone will dare come in.'

'Hang on, Ma,' says Tip suddenly alert. 'I thought you was going to tell Harry our idea – I reckon we should do it tonight, before it's noticed.'

'What idea?' asks Shaw.

'Well, my angel, that was before all this,' replies Milly. 'I ain't at all sure about that, what with the police and everything. Anyway, it need not concern Mr. Bilcher, I'm sure.'

'Ma! He can keep a secret.'

'I can,' states the admirable Bilcher. 'Ask anyone and they will tell you how many secrets I have kept. It's a well-known fact.'

'What idea?' enquires Shaw again.

'I fixed one of the windows,' says Tip, conspiratorially. 'A good shove and I'm in. Easy as anything.'

'Where?' asks Shaw, none the wiser, massaging his temples with his fingers.

'At the Eagle. I fixed the window by the alley. I reckon I could get in.'

Shaw laughs and shakes his head. 'I'm not up to climbing, dear boy, in case you ain't noticed.'

'You'd just keep watch, Harry,' says Tip, grinning at his own ingeniousness, 'and I'd do it.'

'Milly?' says Shaw, uncertainty in his voice. 'Not now, surely? Tell him he can't do it.'

'Well,' she replies thoughtfully, 'now I ain't sure what's best, really I ain't.'

Shaw groans in frustration. 'Wilkes keeps everything locked up. It'll never be worth it.'

Tip grins and interrupts before Milly can reply. 'I know where he keeps the keys.'

'Are you sure?' asks Shaw incredulously.

'Sure as anything. We'll teach him, eh, Harry?'

Shaw bites his tongue but, noticing the glow of pride on Milly's face as she gazes at her son, reluctantly mutters his assent.

'We'd have been better off going with the police,' he says mordantly.

'You just make sure my boy comes to no harm, that's all,' says Milly, giving the boy's head a maternal rub.

Tip squirms.

CHAPTER THIRTY-SEVEN

PARADISE ROW TO RATCLIFFE HIGHWAY

I WILL TALK TO Wilkes, although it will be difficult to get away.

What else can I do?

—

Friday.

When I light the fire in Miss Wallace's room, I learn that she is still complaining of chill, though she looks a little better than previously; she says she will dress herself, but I am not sure she means it. My next task is the Reverend's breakfast, his daily helping of porridge. He takes a long time to eat it, slowly slurping upon each spoonful. When he is finally done, he returns to reading the obituaries in *The Times*. As I clear away the crockery, however, he looks up from the paper and addresses me.

'Thorne, the Society takes me to the lowest regions of this city, as you know, spreading the gospel. '*Go out quickly into the streets and lanes of the city, and bring in hither the poor, and the maimed, and the halt, and the blind.*' That is my lot. Often my daughter, may the Lord bless her, will help me but, as you know, she is indisposed. I am inclined, upon giving the matter some thought, to call upon your assistance.'

'Mine, Sir?'

'Merely to help in distributing the new pamphlet, Thorne, nothing more. It is unfortunate my daughter cannot assist, but the Lord's work cannot be contingent upon our natural frailties. Albert is preparing the carriage – and so I would be grateful if you could ready yourself. We should make an early start.'

I curtsey and take away the breakfast things before dashing upstairs to get my shawl. I can hardly refuse him, though I do not relish the prospect of standing upon a street corner, handing out the Reverend's nonsense. I go back downstairs and find Albert waiting by the carriage.

'Good morning, Flora.'

'Good morning, Albert.'

'I didn't expect you on one of our little jaunts – I hope Miss Wallace ain't too bad in herself.'

'I don't think so. Where are we going?'

'I don't know precisely, but I think it is Whitechapel and Wapping today. Here's the Reverend himself.'

The Reverend Wallace comes down the steps in his full black uniform, his collar tight around his scrawny neck like an ivory manacle. He carries two bundles of papers in his hands and offers me one of them, bidding me to enter the carriage, then giving Albert detailed directions. Once inside, he sits beside me as we set off, staring out of the window at the houses along Church Street.

'Can you read, Thorne?' he says, turning to face me.

'A little, Sir.'

'See what you can make of these,' he says, pulling out one of the sheets from my bundle and handing it to me. I squint at it to indicate my concentration. The contents are reminiscent of what I've already heard from the Reverend, enjoining the poorer classes to better themselves through their personal cleanliness and faith in Christ. I cannot imagine either topic holding much interest in the riverside rookeries, but who am I to disagree?

'I think,' I say hesitantly, after a suitable juncture, 'it has great merit, Sir.'

'In that you are quite correct, Thorne, admirably so. We shall distribute these today, and, as we do so, you must tell the people that there will be a meeting tonight upstairs at the Stepney Tavern. Do you understand?'

'Yes, Sir.'

'Very good.'

He says nothing more. We end up travelling through Shacklewell and Hackney, though I do not know the area well, then a bridge across the canal, and we pass Bethnal Green. The sky is black and gloomy, but the roads are quite dry, and so the carriage jogs swiftly along, progressing south towards the river then turning sharply to the east. It is a region which I recognise, the worst stretch of the Ratcliff Highway near the White Swan. It is not long before Albert pulls the horses to a stop and helps us out of the carriage, though he looks nervous at stopping in such a place. The Reverend does not notice his discomfort; doubtless he is well aware of the Highway's reputation and seeks it out precisely for that reason. I cannot imagine, however, that his pamphlets will effect a considerable change upon the restless population of sailors and whores who live here.

At least he does not give me the papers and despatch me off upon my own: he merely takes my arm and, together, we stroll along the road like a fine pair of fools. There are a few men loitering outside the taverns, many of which are not yet open for the day, and we offer each group our pamphlets. At best they laugh and take a copy of the leaflet, crumpling it up before we have even moved away. Others curse us and a couple of them even spit. Outside the Swan, a little street arab begs for change and, when the Reverend gives her a ha'penny, a gang of twenty or more immediately surround us, pawing at my skirts for several minutes until they tire of the game.

No wonder Miss Wallace is ill. I cannot blame her.

—

You jovial sailors, one and all,
When you are in the port of London call,
Mind Ratcliff Highway and the damsels loose,
The William, The Bear and Paddy's Goose

Lord, where did that spring from?

—

We have been walking for a good hour, and I am merely grateful that we have not been physically harmed, despite several threats to the contrary. Perhaps the Reverend's costume engenders some slight atom of respect or perhaps they are simply used to such do-gooders. The Reverend, meanwhile, seems quite immune to the response he receives; he takes any kind word from his 'flock' as signifying a miraculous conversion to his Hygienic Gospel, and ignores the rest with astounding composure. Moreover, wherever we come to an empty stretch of the road, when there is no unfortunate soul to be saved, he regales me with miniature sermons upon on the merits of teetotalism. He is tireless, and, as I wonder how long I can keep up with him, it becomes a rhetorical question.

'Flora!'

At first, I do not notice it, since I am not so used to my new name. Then I recognise the voice, a voice familiar to me from Wapping.

Maggie.

'Flora – ain't this a pleasant surprise!'

She runs up to us from a side street, dressed in cheap blue silk and dragging a gaggle of her cronies with her. They are already quite drunk, though it is barely eleven o'clock in the morning.

'Thorne?' enquires the Reverend, eyeing me with a sudden suspicion. 'Do you know these unfortunate women?'

'Knows us? Bless her, your Honour, course she knows us. Knows a trick or two, she does, and no mistake, eh, darlin'?'

'I really don't . . .'

'She's just comin' with us for a little while, your Highness,' Maggie says, bowing towards the Reverend Wallace and grabbing my arm tight with her strong fingers. 'Come for a little talk with us, eh, Florrie dear?'

The Reverend looks at me, dismayed by this turn of events; I can see his opinion of me is a little dented. Albert, meanwhile, is not within view and, even if he were, I am not sure he would help me. Maggie attempts to march me into a nearby alley, and her friends are ready to assist her. She is far too strong for me to grapple with.

What can I do?

I twist my head against my arm and bite deep into her hand.

The Reverend looks stunned, but not half as much as my captor, squealing in pain as I break free of her. I push past them both, dodging the traffic and rushing into the narrow lanes on the other side of the Highway. I can still hear them screeching like harpies behind me, and so I keep running through the unfamiliar streets, desperately turning left and right until I am hopelessly lost in the alleys, though I know Whitechapel well enough.

I find a place to hide, a shabby yard separated from the road.

It is not dissimilar to the place where I stopped that night.

Chapter Thirty-Eight

Paradise Row

THAT NIGHT.

I wish I did not remember it so well.

I had completed my day's chores, which were not too demanding, when Ellen came and found me in the kitchen. She seemed a little agitated.

'Nat, did you hear something outside?'

'Something?'

'Someone. I thought I heard someone in the garden.'

'I didn't hear anything. Why don't you ask your Mr. Quill to go and look?'

Quill had been there a month or more. Ellen had never once dropped the pretence that he was simply a hired hand, and I had no better idea of what was going on than when he had first arrived. I wanted her to confide in me, but I knew nothing would persuade her.

'He's got the night off. Lock the door, will you?'

'*I'll* have a look,' I said, taking a poker which I used for the grate in the range, and opening the door. It was dark outside and difficult to make out anything beyond the few shrubs planted by the kitchen wall. The only noise was the creaking of the branches of the oak trees, which lay close to the house.

'Nothing,' I called back.

'Come back inside, and lock the door,' she replied, standing there, watching me anxiously. I followed her instructions, though it was odd to see her so nervous.

'Ellie, what's wrong?'

'Nothing, maybe I'm dreaming it. I thought I saw a man outside, that's all.'

'Well, if there was anyone there, we'll have scared him off. All the windows are shut, ain't they?'

She nodded. 'Stay with us a bit, Nat. We could have a drop of gin, maybe.'

It had been a week or two since she had spoken to me like this, as a friend, not simply a skivvy. I confess, part of me wanted to punish her for it.

'I really must be going. I told Jenkins I'd see him at Collins's. Come with us, if you like.'

'No, I don't want to go out. Won't you stay a while, Nat? I'd feel so much better?'

I reluctantly agreed. We took her lamp, and a bucket more of coal for the fire, and went and sat in the parlour, where I stoked up the flames and she poured the gin. There were a few more homely touches about the place, namely some porcelain she had bought for the mantelpiece, and a new fire-guard. Nonetheless, as she sat down, I did not think she looked very much like the mistress of the house.

'What shall we talk about?' she asked, as she handed me the gin. I decided, foolishly, to try her one last time.

'You. Ellie, tell me what's going on here, with you and Quill, you and this house . . .'

'Nat, don't pry,' she said, scolding me, as if I was a silly little girl.

'Pry? Just tell me what's going on, Ellie. How bad can it be? We used to be friends, didn't we?'

'Leave it, Nat. Please. It's better you don't know.'

'Don't I deserve to know? I'm not some little chit you took from the workhouse, you know. I don't have to cook and clean for you.'

'Perhaps I should let you go then,' she said. Did she mean it as a joke? In retrospect, I think so. At the time, I was too annoyed to think at all.

'You're a heartless bitch, you know that? I'll spare you the bother,' I said, getting up and storming to the door, 'I'm going.'

'Nat!' she said. 'Come back, will you?'

I ignored her and let myself out through the front door, slamming it behind me.

—

Did she have a sense of what was coming?

I think she did, and I abandoned her to it.

—

I made my way down to Albion Road, not really thinking of where I was going, tearful and breathless. I finally came to a halt on Newington Green, sitting on one of the benches in the darkness, wiping my face. How long did I stay there? Half an hour? An hour? I cannot say for certain. A few carriages passed by, heading towards Lower Street; I remember little else. I merely knew that I did not want to leave it like that, and I regretted what I had said almost immediately: Ellen was secretive, thoughtless perhaps, but not malicious. I stayed there, vacillating as to whether I should go back, or wait until the next day. In the end, I straightened my dress and retraced my steps so that, a quarter of an hour later, I stood outside the house once more.

I noticed the front door was ajar almost immediately, but I thought nothing of it and walked into the hall. I called her name, opening the door to the parlour, thinking I would find her sitting there, just as I had left her. Nothing was broken or out of place, except the body upon the rug. It was Ellen's body, lying twisted on the floor like a broken doll, blood staining the torn fabric of her dress, congealing in a dark circle about her midriff. Instinctively, I thought it was some peculiar piece of theatrical foolery, a joke at my expense; I expected her to stand up and take a bow. She did not move. I walked over and bent down, touching her warm face. Still she did not move. I ran my fingers over the damp silk, trying to feel her heart beating. It was a grey silk, London Dust or Navarino.

Nothing.

I sat watching her for some time until the noise of someone descending the stairs roused me. It was Quill, of course, standing in the doorway staring at me, my hands wet with Ellen's blood.

It was then that I ran.

I thought someone would catch me.

He had seen me, after all, hands covered in blood, touching her. Who knows who else might have seen me running from the house? How easy to lay the blame at my feet, if they caught me? How easy to lock me away?

I could not bear that. Moreover, as I ran, the idea spun around my head, that if I had not left her there alone, she might have lived.

I still think so.

Chapter Thirty-Nine

Whitechapel to Shepherdess Walk

I wake in the alley. It is almost dark, and I can only hope that Maggie has given up pursuing me.

Where shall I turn? Impossible to go back to the Reverend Wallace, that much is certain. Perhaps that is for the best.

I will talk to Wilkes, as I planned.

It is a tiresome walk to the City Road. I end up taking a haphazard route through the narrow streets of Whitechapel and then by Shoreditch Church. The night is turning cold, and my stomach grumbles, though I do not have a ha'penny to buy myself food. Worse, I imagine the spectre of Maggie everywhere, conjuring her from every glimpse of some solitary woman lingering in a doorway, or picturing her amongst the gangs of factory girls on their way home. Nevertheless, I finally find myself standing outside the Eagle, gazing at the twin great stone birds that impassively adorn the roof. I venture inside; there are a few men around the bar, but no-one pays any heed to me until I address the man behind the counter.

'I would like to speak with Mr. Wilkes, if you please.'

'And who's calling?' asks the burly man I am addressing, sarcasm in his voice. 'Do you have a calling card?'

'Just tell him it is a message from the Reverend Wallace.'

The man tuts to himself and disappears upstairs. When he returns, he seems a little contrite and beckons me around to the stairs. I follow him to the first floor where we find Arthur Wilkes sitting at his desk writing. He barely glances at me as he speaks.

'Well, it's the new girl is it not?' he says, recognising me from our meeting at the Wallaces'. 'And what business, pray tell, do you have disturbing decent folk at this hour? A message from the old man?'

'There isn't any message. I am afraid I have left the Reverend's employment.'

'Oh my dear. Without a good character? Did you think we might find you something? I fear we have no place for new artistes at the present, my love. Come back in a couple of months.' His amused gaze returns to the papers on his desk, feigning not to notice me any further.

'I've come to talk to you about Ellen Warwick.'

Wilkes looks up, narrowing his slit eyes. 'What about her?'

'I am her sister.'

He looks startled, even more so than the

policeman when I tried the same trick on him.

'She didn't have a sister,' he says sharply. 'What are you playing at?'

'I am her sister,' I say emphatically. 'Did she never mention me to you? We were separated when young and . . .'

'What of it?' he interrupts. 'I see it now – preying on the Reverend's family until he finds you out, coming here. There's nothing for you here, my dear; she left nothing behind but her debts. Owed me plenty, in fact.'

'Debts?'

'Never you mind. There's nothing for you here.'

'I don't want money. I just want to know what happened, who killed her,' I reply angrily.

Wilkes laughs, amused at my temper. 'Both you and the police, I am sure, my dear. Why are you bothering me in particular?'

'Do you know what happened to her diary, do you know who has it?'

Wilkes snorts in derision. 'No I do not, nor do I believe she had the wits to write one. Nor that she had a sister, come to that. Please leave before I ask my friend Simms to eject you,' he says, gesturing in the direction of the burly man who showed me upstairs, who has been standing in the doorway all the while.

This is not going very well. 'Quill killed her, didn't he?'

'Quite the detective in petticoats ain't she, Simms?' he sniggers. 'Leave all that to the police, my dear. Sister or not, she ain't worth your time.'

'I'll be the judge of that.'

'Oh no, I don't think so. I don't think you knew her very well at all, your precious "sister", did you?'

'Not for some years. I was in service in Salisbury.'

'Well, let me share a secret with you, my dear. She was just a whore, an expensive one I admit, but a whore all the same. I set her up in business, you know, but she didn't make anything of it. How do you think she was paying me back, eh?'

He watches me for some reaction. A whore? I have heard something similar said of every woman who worked the theatres. And it is true of some of them, of course.

'It doesn't surprise you?' he asks, teasing me. 'I thought you had something of the gutter about you.'

'No more than you, I expect. Ellen wasn't like that.'

'Oh, she spits fire, this one, does she not, Mr. Simms? Wait there, my girl, just you wait there.'

I stand there as he scuttles to a locked cabinet in the corner of the room and pulls out a bunch of keys to open one of the drawers. He brings out a hand-tooled leather case, decorated with delicate needlework, and opens it, placing it in front of me. It holds a daguerreotype, glinting in the light, which I have to tilt slightly to see the silvery image. It is what they call an 'artistic' work, a woman lying naked on rumpled sheets, her head twisted coyly over her shoulder, smiling into the camera.

'Do you recognise her, my dear?'

Lord. He is right – it is Ellen.

'Not one of her best, but still a pretty picture, is it not?'

'You had her do this?' I ask, finding it difficult to take in what he is telling me.

'Ha! Had her do it? Oh that's a good one, I made her! You're not listening to me, are you now?' he says, touching my cheek with his bony fingers. 'She was for hire, my dear, ready and willing. Quite beautiful, I'll admit, quite cunning. Still a whore for all that. We had quite a nice arrangement, until she . . . well, you know how it is.'

He sits down again, chuckling at my discomfort, keen to increase it.

'That is one of the early photographs, I believe. Quite an artist was Mr. Quill, quite a photographic talent, would you not say?'

'Quill?' I ask in astonishment.

'You don't know much about anything, do you, Miss?'

'You're lying,' I say, still in a daze, touching the velvet lining of the daguerreotype case. 'She was an artist's model; it means nothing.'

'Oh, it was quite *artistic*, my dear. You should see some of her more intimate studies, yes indeed, very romantic. I would oblige but all of them went to the clients who requested them, by and large. Collector's items, you see? Well, it's been a pleasure, I am sure – please don't call again.'

He waves his hand dismissing me, chuckling to himself, and the man he called Simms grabs me, pulling me back downstairs.

'Whore!' I hear Wilkes shouting merrily like a lunatic.

'Whore!'

Chapter Forty

Shepherdess Walk

It is much later that same night when Tip and Shaw dash down the alley that runs beside the Eagle, dodging the puddles and the horse dung. As they shelter from the rain, huddling together beside the old stables that adjoin the main building, the bell of St. Luke's chimes for three o'clock. Shaw looks up at the sky; there is no moon and little chance that they might be seen. All the same, they wait there, standing in the darkness like statues.

'No-one around,' whispers Shaw. 'Well? Where is it?'

'Up there,' says the boy, pointing to the dim outline of the elaborate stucco cornice that adorns the corner of the building.

'That won't hold your weight.'

'I reckon it will.'

'And I reckon your mother will murder me if you kill yourself,' he whispers hurriedly.

'But then I'll be dead, and I won't care. Give us a bunk up.'

Shaw swears under his breath, rubbing his

weary shoulders with his hand, feeling the bruises still on his back.

'Be quick about it then,' he says, cupping his hands together to grab the boy's foot, and leans back against the wall.

The boy does not hesitate, scrabbling over Shaw, narrowly missing his face with his boots, and springs up onto the ledge that surrounds the first floor. From that vantage, he inches his way gradually around the building until he comes to a large sash window that overlooks the landing inside. He pushes it upwards, slowly but forcefully, and it easily gives a good half inch, since the screws holding the latch are not quite as tight as intended. Tip smiles at his own handiwork and bends down, pulling a small iron jemmy from inside his jacket, which he wedges between the frame and the window. He kneels down on top of it and forces it with his foot, increasing the pressure until the latch clips free of the frame and the window slides open. He does not move, however, but waits on the ledge in case anyone has heard the noise. When he is confident that no-one is coming, he slips inside, carefully closing the window behind him.

Shaw paces nervously up and down the alley, alternating between watching the street and peering anxiously up at the building. The rain has died down, but he is cold and wet and longs to return to the relative comfort of Bilcher's attic or, ideally, Milly Lampton's tender embrace.

It is a good ten minutes until he hears the window being rattled open once more; in fact, it makes such a noise that he is surprised at Tip being so clumsy. He hears the boy's voice, urgent and hoarse, calling his name.

'What's going on?' whispers Shaw anxiously.

The boy climbs out onto the ledge and jumps recklessly down into the alley, not waiting for any assistance, landing expertly on his feet. Shaw reaches for him in the darkness, managing to grab the collar of his jacket and swing him round.

'What's going on?' he says again, more insistently, breathing into the boy's face.

'Run, just run, or we're for it.'

'Run?'

Tip darts off without warning, and Shaw, cursing, follows him as best as he is able. Even if he were in the best of health, he could not match the speed of his partner. He jogs breathlessly along the darkened streets that branch from the City Road, the boy waiting for him at every corner, urging him onwards. Finally, they slump together, exhausted, in another passage, equally dark and full of muck, not far from Smithfield Market.

The night is still black as coal, and both man and boy seem like a mere shadow to each other.

'What happened?' asks Shaw, his tone both pleading and accusatory.

'I didn't mean to . . .' stammers the boy, 'but he went for me.'

'Who did? What do you mean?' Shaw's voice ranges towards panic.

'It was Wilkes, he must have woke up. He came

at me with something in his hand. A knife.' He stops, almost tearful. 'I only meant to trip him up.'

'And?'

'I think I killed him. I think he was dead when I hooked it.'

'Killed?' Shaw murmurs, shocked. 'Did anyone see you?'

'No, I don't think so. Weren't no-one else about.'

'Then you weren't never there, do you hear? Not even if your Ma asks you. Do you understand, my boy?'

'Never there?'

'We never went near the place. Spent the night at a tavern down by the river instead. You can't recall the name, right?'

'It weren't my fault.'

'That doesn't matter,' replies Shaw. 'It's what other people think that counts. Let's see those clothes,' he says, grabbing the boy by the shoulders and twisting him towards the light coming from the distant street lamps.

'No blood,' whispers Shaw to himself, thankfully. 'Let's keep moving then.'

Chapter Forty-One

Little White Lion Street

The rain has stopped as Tip and Shaw trudge wearily up the slope of Snow Hill but there is a fog rolling in from the river. By the time they reach Little White Lion Street, though it is several hours from daylight, the early morning crowds of beggars, hawkers and children are already filling the smoky streets that radiate from Seven Dials. Shaw knocks briskly on Bilcher's door, damning him under his breath as they wait in the cold. Eventually, Bilcher appears and ushers them inside, ascending the narrow stairs that wind up three floors to the attic room.

'Did it come off?' asks Bilcher, eagerly.

'No,' says Shaw, perhaps too quickly, 'we couldn't get in.'

'Milly won't be happy,' adds Bilcher.

'Hmm,' says Shaw.

'I'll be in the shop, if you need anything,' says Bilcher, and, perceiving that Shaw will not be supplying further details, he turns to go back downstairs. Once he is sure that Bilcher has left, Shaw paces the room, only pausing to scan the street from the window.

'We'll have to lay low somewhere, you know that?' he says to Tip. 'We can't wait here.'

The boy scowls. 'Leave the Dials? Ma won't like it.'

'I'll find somewhere, somewhere out of the way,' continues Shaw, ignoring the boy. 'I used to have some pals in Tottenham, maybe we can look them up.'

'I'm going to tell Ma,' says the boy, getting up.

'No you ain't,' replies Shaw, jumping to the door and slamming it shut. 'We ain't showing our faces, no more than we have to, anyway. I say we don't mention a word to anyone, not even your blessed Ma. If no-one knows, they can't tell, can they?'

Tip shrugs. 'Maybe.'

'Do you want your Ma to see you swing, strung up like a piece of beef?'

'No.'

'Well then, just you pay heed to me. We'll wait till it's dark again and set off.'

Tip says nothing but sits down, kicking the table.

'They'll find him dead – Ma will guess we did it.'

'Let her. We don't say anything, right?'

The boy nods.

—

Night turns into day imperceptibly; the morning light is so dimmed by the fog that the inhabitants of the Dials barely notice the difference. Shaw and Tip, meanwhile, sit quietly in the room, staring at the bare walls of the attic; neither can find a source of amusement or conversation in their predicament, and so they say nothing. Bilcher does not return for some time, but, when he does, he is accompanied by Milly Lampton.

'Well, this is a fine look-out, I must say,' she states, striding into the room.

'Milly,' says Shaw, 'before you say anything, I've decided – we must get away, make sure the police don't have us.'

'What?' she says.

'I've thought it through, and it ain't safe, my love. Not for me, nor the boy.'

'What about Wilkes? Have you given up already?'

'Well, we didn't get in this time,' replies Shaw, 'and it's not sensible going back. Listen to me, Milly, we've got to hook it, sharp as we can. I think there'll be trouble if we don't, honest.'

'It ain't like you to take on like this, Harry,' she says, mystified by his sudden anxiety. 'And what am I to do by myself without my boy?'

'We'll come back in a month or two,' says Shaw, 'when things have blown over.'

He tries to clasp her hand, but she snatches it away petulantly and stands next to Tip's seat, stroking his matted hair.

'And what will become of you, my angel?' she says.

'I'll be all right, Ma.'

Milly looks doubtful. 'And what do I tell the crushers when they come calling?'

'It's better you don't know nothing, Milly, honest.'

'It'd be better if we didn't know you, Harry Shaw; that's all I can say,' she exclaims, pulling a handkerchief from her sleeve and blowing her nose vigorously. 'You've been nothing but trouble for us, since the first day we clapped eyes on you.'

'Milly!' he exclaims, imploringly.

'You heard me – taking liberties, taking my boy away,' she sobs tearfully. 'It ain't right and don't expect me to be grateful; 'cos I ain't.'

'We'll go tonight then,' says Shaw, resigned.

Milly sobs further, kissing her son on the cheek and running to the door weeping. 'They'll be wondering where I've got to. I'll come back later.'

'Don't worry Ma,' says Tip. 'They won't catch us.'

Shaw watches her leave and closes the door behind her. Bilcher, having observed the whole conversation, shakes his head.

'She's a tartar, ain't she?'

Shaw frowns at him. 'Do you think you might find us some food?'

—

It is almost noon, and Shaw dozes in his chair, having given up on keeping watch through the window. Tip does not sleep, however, but merely squats dejectedly against the brickwork of the attic, playing with the cobwebs and watching Shaw's face as he snores. When he is satisfied that Shaw is slumbering soundly, he gets up and cautiously tiptoes to the door, raising the latch and letting himself out.

Step by step, the boy creeps down the stairs to

the street door and from there into the narrow alley beside the Lion. It is a simple matter for him to clamber over the wall and let himself into the kitchen, and, with equal aplomb, he avoids the bar, where he can hear his mother talking, and makes his way upstairs to his room.

In all honesty, it is little more than a cell, a meagre space graced only with a mattress and chest of drawers, but it is his home, and he has some fondness for it. He steps out onto the landing, checking that his mother is still downstairs and then returns, loosening the bricks beside the fireplace and pulling out his box of treasures, looking for a particular couple of items.

Chapter Forty-Two

Abney Park

I SPEND THE NIGHT wandering the streets; I am too cold to stop walking, and my mind is too restless. Only the occasional carriage passes me by, and a few men and women on foot, as abject and friendless as myself. It was Ellen in the photograph, of course, but, as to the rest, I can hardly believe it of her.

There is a thick fog in the morning, as bad as the night she died, and I can only think of one place to go.

—

The fog still hangs choking in the air, occluding the twin obelisks that guard the cemetery. I should be grateful since, if the gatekeeper could see me well enough to make out the damp and dirt on my clothes, I doubt he would let me through. I wander down towards the chapel in the mist, passing by the neatly tended graves until I find Ellen's headstone. There are some wilting flowers laid from previous days but nothing fresh. The stone is terribly cold as I bend down and touch it.

'She was a beautiful woman, like you, she was.'

The voice wakes me from my reverie. It is Daniel Quill: he sits a few feet behind me, half-hidden in the bushes, swigging something from a flask. I would guess it is gin, since I can almost smell his breath better than I can see him. He looks like he has been there all night.

'I come here every day, but I haven't seen you before,' he says, slurring every other word and smiling inanely, a peculiar contrast to the mannered condescension I remember. 'Two shillings for a quick ride, perhaps, little Miss?' he says unashamedly, fumbling in his pockets.

I should expect no better, I suppose. However, he walks so unsteadily I doubt he could even undo his belt. I smile sweetly and take his arm.

'Let's find somewhere quieter,' I say, leading him gently away towards the outer circle of cemetery, trying to stop him falling with every step.

'Did you know her, Miss Warwick, I mean?' I ask ingenuously after we have walked a few feet, nodding back to the tombstone.

'She was beautiful, a beautiful woman,' he mumbles, taking another swig of the gin.

'How did you know her, then?'

He grins at me again, reaching inaccurately inside his jacket and, eventually, retrieving a wallet from which he pulls a silvery sheet. 'Look,' he says emphatically, practically pulling my head off its shoulders as he attempts to draw my face to within an inch of the item in question: it is Ellen, another daguerreotype, naked again but for some diaphanous cloth draped over her chest, her head posed coquettishly on her shoulder, avoiding the gaze of the camera.

'It's mine,' he says.

'I can see that,' I reply, not wanting to believe it.

'No, I did it, you see?' he says with slurred pride. 'I took the photograph.'

'Is that your profession?'

He laughs, leaning on me. 'It might be that it is. Sittings for all shapes and sizes, a bit like yourself, my dear. Come on now,' he mumbles, 'come on, stop playing me around. Where are we going?'

I push him off gently, but I can't think of a clever way to tackle him. 'Was it Wilkes? Did he make her do them?'

It sounds blunt and stupid, and I regret saying it. He switches immediately to a voice that is suspicious and sharp. Perhaps he is not so drunk as all that.

'Who are you?' he asks, grabbing me tight. We are somehow back at the tall cedar that stands in the heart of the cemetery.

'My name's Flora . . . I used to know Ellen some time ago, that's all. I just thought . . .'

'Well, you thought wrong, my dear. She wasn't anybody's fool, not her. It was her idea, the photographs, everything. Quite a business. I tried to get her out of it but ...'

His voice trails off, his hands wander to grab my rear, squeezing for amusement or support, I cannot tell which. His breath still reeks of the stale liquor. 'What do you mean everything?' I ask, trying to ignore his grip as he begins to fumble with my skirt.

'You know the things men like, my dear. I'm sure you do. Fancies for particular clothing or seeing this or that, here or there. Come on now, don't be shy; I'll demonstrate,' he suggests, leering, oblivious to our location, pulling up at my skirts ineffectually.

'You mean you took pictures of her for money?' I ask breathless, turning my head to avoid his kisses.

'To suit every taste,' he whispers in my ear, still mauling my behind, planting wet lips on my neck. 'How do you like it, darling? I can give it to you however you like.'

'Did you kill her?' I whisper.

'No,' he says, stopping short. There is a tremor of anxiety in his voice. 'I loved her.'

'Wilkes then? Was he there? Someone else?'

He stops mauling me, extracting his hands from my skirts and steps back aghast, every movement exaggerated by the drink. 'The police sent you, didn't they?'

He looks around wildly, clearly fearful of something. Miraculously, no-one else has come by this spot.

'Don't be scared,' I say trying to calm him, 'there are no police . . . Just tell me if Wilkes was there.'

'I don't care about the police, you little fool,' he whispers, suddenly sounding quite sober. 'It's the bloody devil that killed her. It'll be you next if you're not careful, you just wait.'

'What?'

'He's following me; I know he is. He's gone and

done the others already. One by one.'

'What others? What are you talking about? You know who killed her?' I ask incredulously.

'Not just her, Aspenn for one: he's had it. It was in the papers.'

'You know who killed her?' I say, desperately re-iterating the question.

'I saw him outside once, and I didn't think anything of it. He was there, when I found her. I know he was,' he whispers, more to himself than to me.

He starts to run off, doing up his belt as he goes, and almost topples over in the process.

'Who? Who did you see?'

He looks terrified, backing away from me.

'Who?' I shout, barely catching up with him.

'The boy. He watched the house, you see?' he says, gesturing in the direction of Church Street. 'He was watching us all the time we . . .'

His train of thought stops abruptly as he runs off. I can barely see him, swallowed up by the fog. Only the drunken diminished sound of his voice carries through the air. 'Don't stay here. It isn't safe here. Not anywhere near.'

'What does he look like?' I shout, running after him to no avail.

Silence. Lying on the path, however, is the photograph of Ellen he showed me. He must have dropped it in his hurry – no doubt he has others.

I pick it up and look at her.

Strangely, it is quite beautiful.

Chapter Forty-Three

Shepherdess Walk and Seven Dials

THE BANGING ON the doors wakes her, a repetitive thumping knock, and raised voices downstairs. She stretches her back, old bones clicking into place, and peers into the gloom, finding comfort in the familiar jumble of objects.

'Arthur?' Jemima says, straining to get up from the chair.

There is no answer. She hobbles into the corridor and tries his room, but the bed is quite empty, the sheets crumpled and pulled to one side. Tentatively, she wanders further along and begins to descend the stairs, clutching the rail tight as she makes her way down to the first floor. She does not notice the broken lock on the landing window, only that the door to her brother's office is ajar. She expects to find him there at the desk as usual, engrossed in some obscure calculation, but, rather, he is there lying prone on the floor, his nightgown slashed open about his stomach, the skin sliced and folded out on itself like pastry, encrusted with dried blood. She turns around again, hearing the banging at the doors to the pub once more, and slowly walks downstairs.

'Arthur?' she says.

Tip lines up the complete contents of his hoard upon the floorboards of his room. A black diary, a daguerreotype, his hoard of miniature photographs, a leather wallet, a pair of gold cuff-links, a cigar box. He opens the diary, takes up a rough pencil he keeps in his jacket and scans the pages, crossing out the word 'Wilkes' wherever he sees it. He does not understand the rest quite so well, especially the numbers, but he can read the names well enough. He feels happy with his progress.

After he has been through every page, scoring through numerous entries, he shuts the book and looks once more at the daguerreotype: Ellen Warwick, her body stretched out, legs apart, smiling vacantly at the man who crouches over her. A gentleman in full evening dress is in the foreground with his back to the camera, carefully placed in the photograph but with his face deliberately hidden. The boy recognises him easily, however. He remembers hiding himself and watching them take the photograph, the man squatting there like a grotesque statue.

He throws the picture onto the fire and stokes the coals which his mother has left burning. Even though they are barely warm, the shiny surface shrivels up quickly enough. He flicks through the *Darlings of the London Stage* and then finds his best picture of Ellen; she looks like when he first saw her, before everything was spoiled.

He gathers up the remaining objects and,

instead of replacing them in the box, stuffs them inside his jacket. As quietly as he came in, he makes his way downstairs and out into the alley. Bilcher is busy with a customer, and so he deftly slips behind him and back up the steps that lead to the attic.

Shaw is where he left him, snoring heavily. The boy studies him for a few seconds then retrieves the cigar box and cuff-links from his pocket, along with a small handkerchief, which he uses to wrap them together. He has practised the art of picking pockets with Shaw on many an occasion, if not with great success. Fortunately, however, Shaw's jacket is hanging half over the chair, the lining turned outwards and a pocket clearly visible, ideal for hiding the little bundle. Cautiously, he bends down beside him and slips the crumpled piece of cloth inside. Shaw nods in his sleep, disturbed by the movement, and one eye gradually opens as, half conscious, he pulls the jacket tight round his stomach.

'What you looking at?'

'Nothing,' says the boy.

He waits some minutes until he is sure that Shaw is asleep again, then once more leaves the room. He goes very slowly, taking great pains not to make a sound as he descends the stairs and closes the door behind himself. This time, he walks off briskly down the street. The fog is beginning to lift as he walks past the front of the Lion and up to the Dials. There, he turns onto Great Earl Street and ambles casually along until he finds a small gang of dirty young children, none older than ten years, chalking shapes on a wall. He recognises a couple of them as regular deposits outside the Lion on occasions when their mother takes a fancy to gin.

'Who wants a shilling?' he asks.

'A shilling?' they chorus, eyes wide. 'What for?' says the most precocious of the bunch.

'Taking a message and keeping it a secret,' he replies.

'Where?'

'Ah,' says Tip, 'that's the thing . . .'

The crowd that fills the Eagle when Jemima Shaw opens the doors is the regular mixture found at midday: the gang of barmen, ready for their shift, and the clientele, ready for their drink, and, although they think it peculiar to see her in such circumstances, they do not pay it much heed. Instead they treat her merely as a regular fixture of the place, since all of them have seen her wandering the establishment at some point. They manage to ignore her for a good hour or more. It is only when her enquiries after her brother become more importunate that one man offers to go up and fetch him. His scream draws others, men and women who pile up the stairs in a frenzy of curiosity, crowding around the doorway to Wilkes's office.

Eventually, someone goes to fetch the police.

Chapter Forty-Four

Scotland Yard to Seven Dials

Inspector Burton *sits* brooding in his office by candlelight. His left cheek is somewhat swollen and scratched, from where one of the female residents of the Dials drew blood, but, otherwise, he is relatively unharmed. It startles him, however, when Johnson rushes into the room without knocking.

'We've got him, Sir,' says Sergeant Johnson, triumphantly.

'Who?'

'This Shaw character, begging your pardon, Sir. Message from St. Giles Station House – someone's tipped them the wink.'

'How so? That's not like the Dials, is it?'

'True, Sir, true, normally they is tight-lipped about their own, but maybe this gentleman ain't got so many friends as he thinks . . . some little street arab came in and passed on the message, so they said.'

'From whom?'

'Said he didn't know. A young gentleman, he said.'

'Hmm. How many lads can they spare?'
'A dozen waiting your orders, sir.'
'That should do it,' says Burton. 'Tell them to get ready and that we'll do it swift this time.'

—

Shaw wakes with a start, the room quite black. Milly Lampton stands beside him, violently shaking his arm, her diminutive form unusually imposing.
'Where is he? What've you done with him? God help me, Harry Shaw, if you've sent him off somewhere on his own without telling me . . .'
'What?' he mumbles, not entirely certain of her meaning.
'Tip! He's not here, is he?'
Shaw looks around, troubled, and forced to agree with her.
'No, he is not, my dear.'
'Don't you "dear" me, Harry – just when I thought it can't get no worse, you manage to drive my boy away.'
'I haven't driven him anywhere . . . He'll be back, he always comes back . . . He knows we've got to leave tonight, anyhow, like we agreed. He wouldn't leave without saying goodbye to *you*, would he now?'
He looks at her and does his best to smile convincingly. She softens a little. 'I suppose you're right. God help us if not, that's all I can say.'
Shaw sits up and pulls her close to him, surprised that she does not object. 'It'll all blow over in a week or two, Milly, then we'll both come back.'

She smiles, but, before he can respond, they both hear the sounds from the street and instinctively go over to the window. The boots on the cobbled stones echo down the road, and then the flash of the bull's-eye lanterns, a dozen or more swinging left and right, scattering light through the evening mist.

'Well, we knew they'd be back. We should be all right here,' says Shaw, trying to convince himself. The sound of the door downstairs being broken through disrupts his line of thought.

'They're coming straight up here,' says Milly, incredulously.

Shaw looks around and jumps to the door, slotting the latch into place, with a speed that belies his age and ill health. The only other way out is a rear window, which opens onto the sloping roof of the building. Without even thinking, he slides it open and begins to clamber outside.

'I haven't killed no-one, you know that?'

Milly merely nods as the police bang on the door; suddenly they break into the room, a half-dozen burly constables and the figure of Inspector Burton. They ignore Milly Lampton and rush to the window, peering out at Shaw as he stands there on the ledge, cursing the fact that it leads him nowhere.

'I'll jump,' he says, looking back at them over his shoulder, standing closer to the edge.

Burton smiles and says casually, 'Let him jump if he likes.'

Shaw curses again and, as he ponders his

options, one of the constables is quick enough to grab his arm and drag him back into the attic. Milly looks at him pityingly.

'Henry Shaw,' says Burton, stroking his beard with pleasure, 'we are placing you under arrest on suspicion of murder.'

They lead him quickly downstairs, keen to avoid a crowd this time, and out along Little White Lion Street, towards St. Giles. Shaw is too weak to protest, and his departure is only watched by the children that play upon the street.

A hundred yards or so down the street, Tip Lampton crouches invisibly in a doorway, watching the procession of lanterns and uniforms go past.

He dare not laugh, but he allows himself a smile.

Inspector Burton sits in the kitchen of the St. Giles Station House enjoying a piping hot cup of coffee. On the table are the contents of Shaw's pockets, laid out ready to be placed in an envelope as evidence. In particular there are two items of which, when searched, the man in question vehemently disclaimed all knowledge.

'Gold cuff-links?' says Burton.

'Matches the description of Aspenn's footman, Sir,' replies Johnson, knowingly.

'Well, we must have him take a look at them in the morning, must we not? Now, what about this cigar box?'

'Well, Sir, you notice there is an inscription "*A. W.*" in the corner?'

'Yes?'

'Well, we don't know as yet, Sir, but it is a mighty fine clue, ain't it?'

Burton smiles smugly and concurs. Meanwhile, a constable walks into the room to obtain his nightly cup of coffee from the stove.

'Suprised to see you here, if I may say so, Inspector,' says the man.

Burton looks at him. 'How do you mean?'

'Well, with that incident at the Eagle – I thought that would be right up your street. The newspapers are crawling all over the place.'

'Incident?'

'Murder, most likely burglary as well. Constable Figgis reckons it's the same bleeder what you're looking for.'

'We have our man, Constable – when did this happen? Why wasn't I informed?'

'Last night, by all accounts, I think, Sir – didn't find the body until this afternoon.'

'Do we know the victim?'

'Oh yes, Sir, that's the thing – Arthur Wilkes himself, the owner.'

Burton's jaw drops, whereas Johnson takes a few moments to register the significance of the news.

'*A.W.*, Sir?'

'Priceless, Johnson, is it not?' says Burton. 'Absolutely priceless. We have our man, all right.'

Chapter Forty-Five

Paradise Row

What do I make of Quill? He was drunk, and yet why should he invent stories for me?

Now what? I am cold and hungry, and I have nowhere to go.

The fog makes it easy enough to slip quietly into the garden by the front gate. I creep beside the wall, circumnavigating the house. The carriage is not on the path, suggesting that the Reverend is not at home, but there are lights in several of the windows, obscured by blinds and shutters.

What can I say, if I see Miss Wallace? That I am not a scheming whore? That I have come to warn her about Quill's supposed murderer? At best, they will think me mad.

I stay hidden in the garden, pondering it for far too long. The damp in the soil begins to seep slowly into my boots. In the end, I must make a dash for the kitchen door or freeze: it is locked, as I expected, but fortunately the key was one of the few things which I had about me when Maggie caught up with us in Whitechapel. I open the door tentatively. There is no-one inside, and the range is on. I ignore the mess that my feet leave on the floor and squat by the stove warming my hands, grateful for the heat, heedless of anything else. There is no sound from upstairs, thankfully, and I stay in that spot for a good half hour, until I think of food and retrieve some cold cuts of ham from the larder.

I have not slept for nearly two days.

I wake up with a start, my neck stiff and painful, forgetful of where I am. Albert, rotund as ever, sits at the opposite end of the kitchen table watching me closely, as he scoffs from a platter of cold meat, continuing where I left off.

'Hallo, Flora,' he says, managing to imbue even these two simple words with a tone of disapproval.

'Hallo,' I reply, weakly.

'I didn't take you for a thief as well as a liar,' he says, piously, looking pointedly at the plate in front of me and the half-eaten food.

'Do I not work here, then?'

'I think you know the answer to that. Lord knows why you've come back here. What do you think the Reverend would say?'

'I'm no fallen woman, whatever you may have heard.'

'That wouldn't matter so much with the Reverend: he's a fair man. As a matter of fact, he is mighty generous to them what he calls his "soiled doves". It is the lies about your character he objects to, I reckon. That letter you had Miss Wallace write for you came back, you see. No such address.'

'I'm sorry.'

'I've taken those keys off you, and I'll be grateful if you leave,' he says sternly.

'I've nowhere to go, Albert,' I reply, doing my best to sound endearing.

'You should have thought of that before.'

'I had nowhere to go then, either. Besides, I must speak to the Reverend.'

'That won't do you no good. Anyhow, it's too late for that tonight.'

'What time is it?'

'Ten o'clock or thereabouts.'

'You mean I've been here all day?'

'You looked like you needed rest,' he says, blushing. 'Nevertheless, the Reverend won't have you here so . . .'

'Have you asked him? Perhaps I could stay the night and talk in the morning,' I interject.

Albert sighs. 'I don't need to ask him, Flora. I'm sorry it's turned out badly for you, but . . .'

He stops because he hears it too. A shriek from upstairs, a man's voice, and then a woman's scream, muffled but distinct enough to be heard. Albert's reaction is immediate, and, as he bounds up the stairs, his speed belies his bulky frame. I follow on behind, though he breathlessly bids me to remain in the kitchen, and I pursue him upstairs to the rear bedroom. I follow Albert through the door, but nothing is as I expected.

The room is lit by two dozen or more candles, scattered around the floor and upon shelves, looking like some theatrical grotto. At one end, near the door, is a box mounted on a tripod, a camera of some sort, I would guess. At the other is a shower bath, one of the peculiar upright tin devices in which water sprays down from a perforated cistern. Miss Wallace stands there, bony and naked in the metal tub, water streaming down her face as she sobs hysterically. We are surrounded by pictures of her, some framed, some lying, perhaps recently developed, upon the floor, all featuring her bathing herself or carrying water. I pick one up, and find it bears a motto, pasted onto the back: *Cleanliness is the supreme duty of woman! Wash your sin away! Bathe in the water of redemption.* Lord. This is his secret work! Does he intend to hand this out on the Ratcliff Highway as well?

I do not think Miss Wallace even sees me, and the sight of her is so unreal that I do not realise what Albert is doing. Crouched down on the floor by her feet, he is shaking something. Only when I move closer, stepping cautiously between the candles, can I see it is the Reverend himself, slumped over the bath. Blood is leaking into the tub from a gaping wound in his stomach, slowly covering his daughter's feet in a dilute pool of crimson. Albert is doing no good, and, each time he tries to aid the old man, a fresh red stream issues from his prone body.

'Who did this?' I ask, grabbing Miss Wallace by the shoulders, forcing her to look at me.

She is crying, half choking as she speaks. 'It was a boy, a street boy. He said that it was for Ellen Warwick, that he shouldn't have . . . that he shouldn't have . . .'

She falters as she looks down at her father but still she does not move, rigid like a statue, her tears mingling with water and the blood. I pass her nightgown to her, which is on a stand by her side. She clutches it as if she has no concept of its function. Albert also seems dazed, but her voice somehow rouses him.

'Where did he go?' he asks, urgently.

She raises a trembling arm towards the stairs, pointing upwards. He releases his grip on the Reverend and rushes out into the hall, bounding up to the attic. The old man is beyond help, so I cannot blame him. But why would this boy go upstairs, unless he wants to be trapped? Or has a way out?

I rush to the window and pull open the shutters. It is dark, but I can see him there well enough, clambering down the tree, a boy of thirteen years or so, agile as a monkey. Albert will not catch him, that much is certain. It explains how he entered the house at will: no-one would check the attic windows, no-one would think it possible.

What now? I will not recognise the boy again: it is too dark to make out anything more than his height. I watch closely through the glass, waiting to see which way he goes: he jumps from the tree but lands badly, clutching at his ankle and limping slightly as he heads for the wall, towards Paradise Bridge.

Miss Wallace screams again, hysterical and frozen, and I hesitate to leave her there, even though I know Albert will look after her. And yet, I came back here for Ellen, not for her.

For the second time in as many weeks, I run from this wretched house.

Chapter Forty-Six

Seven Dials to Paradise Row

Milly Lampton wanders disconsolately around the first floor of the Little White Lion carrying a single candle, her diminutive form flitting like a little ghost between her bedroom and that of her son. In all honesty, Shaw's arrest does not concern her half so much as the boy's absence, and, even though most of Seven Dials is sleeping, she will still stay awake in hope of catching him on his return, her eyes destined to be bloodshot by the morning.

She is so thankful the police did not find him, at least. When he returns, she decides, she will make him a treat for his breakfast.

John Bilcher sleeps soundly in his bed, dreaming of Milly Lampton and the Little White Lion and the tragic death of Harry Shaw. He feels some guilt at the latter imagining, but this is easily assuaged as he pictures himself in charge of the new establishment, a bizarre mixture of Bilcher's Urban Comestibles and said public house, where fruit and vegetables are dished out in pint pots.

When he wakes, he thinks of Milly Lampton still; she will need a new man when Shaw is found to be a murderer.

And hanged by the neck.

Poor Harry.

—

Harry Shaw sits wide awake in his cell. They will move him to Newgate tomorrow, so they say. This does not disturb him in itself, since he has spent some time in gaol before and knows that he can survive it; he may even meet an old acquaintance or two. He is fretting, however, about the so-called evidence that the police seem to have placed upon his person, the cuff-links and the cigar box. If they are so determined to set him up as guilty, what can he do to defend himself?

They have not found the boy, he is sure of that, otherwise they would be boasting of it. Perhaps he got wind of their arrival and that is why he left?

He is glad of that, at least. Milly will be grateful.

Harry Shaw lies back on his bed and wonders whether he can escape the noose.

—

Jemima Shaw snores alone in her chair, comforted by the small dog that lies quietly in her lap. The policeman and attorney have both spoken to her, enquiring after deeds and wills and other matters she cannot understand, but they have decided it best to leave her there for the moment, until a qualified physician might pronounce on her health, both mental and physical, the following day.

She wakes intermittently during the night, calling out for her brother, but he does not answer.

At one point, she recalls vaguely that she once had a husband; she wonders where he is now.

Melody Wallace sits in her bedroom, looking at her feet, playing with the material of her nightgown. Albert has gone to raise the alarm, and so she sits there alone, wondering what she can say to the police to make them understand her father's work. She knows they will not understand the photographs.

She begins to cry again and does not stop.

Chapter Forty-Seven

Green Lanes

I run along Paradise Row, as far as the bridge that crosses the New River. The fog has lifted a little, and the moon can be glimpsed through the clouds, but I can see no trace of the boy. I take the path that goes by the water; it is a dirt track, and, if he is nearby, I fear he must hear my boots splashing in the mud.

I have been this way before, of course.

I come to Green Lanes, where the water disappears through a culvert running underneath the road. I cross to the other side, where it re-emerges and flows down to Canonbury. They are building new houses nearby, and much of the ground hereabouts has been turned into brickfields, a wasteland of building works, kilns and heaped earth. I peer through the darkness, thinking it must be a futile effort, until I see something moving beside the river.

After a hundred yards or so, walking carefully along the bank, I can see him in the distance or, rather, a dark shadow that matches the figure I saw in the garden. I can just make out that he is limping slightly, which perhaps explains how I have managed to catch up.

But what am I to do now that I have him?

My musings become irrelevant, as he disappears around the bend in the river, and, suddenly, I can no longer make him out at all. I run faster along the bank, hoisting up my skirts, desperate to stick with him. I only realise my mistake as he catches me, stretching out from the long grass to trip my legs. He is only a boy, thirteen perhaps, but he is quick and strong enough to pin me down with ease; he lands on top of me with a thump.

'Why are you followin' me?' he asks, pulling out a small rough-edged blade and holding it to my neck. The metal is ice cold against my skin. I am not sure what I can say to him.

'You know why – you realise you've killed him?'

'He was in the book, weren't he?' he says, wiping the blade against my neck, trying to scare me. He is succeeding. What book?

'And Ellen? What about her?'

He looks strangely vexed. He wasn't expecting that.

'Who are you?'

'You killed her, didn't you?'

'What do you know about it?' he says petulantly, like a child.

'I know you did it.'

'So?' he replies, drawing the knife so tight against my skin that I fear that he has drawn blood.

'Why?'

'Why?' he says, incredulous, as if the answer

would be obvious to a simpleton. 'It was disgusting, what she was doing. Everyone looking at her like that.'

'You mean the pictures?'

'I used to watch her, see? Look,' he says, reaching with one hand inside his pocket. He pulls out a little piece of card, a commercial *carte de visite*, one of the ones which Ellen had made for the mourning business. 'She gave me that. Ma used to take me to see her.'

'But you murdered her.'

'I just wanted to see her again,' he says, frowning, 'so I follows her. But she was always in the house, in that room. It was disgusting what she did with them.'

'Worse than what you've been doing?'

He ignores me. 'She wouldn't stop doing it. I went and asked her, but she wouldn't. Said she'd tell the Peelers on me. I put a stop to that. And you ain't going to tell on me.'

He raises his hand with the knife. I have a flash of inspiration.

'What about Quill?'

He pauses. Lord. He would have killed me.

'I know him – the one what took the pictures. He's in her book too.'

He has the diary. That is what happened to it. He is taking the names from the diary – did she pose for Wallace as well, was that why he went for him? Or was it just seeing his ludicrous photography?

'Yes, what about Quill? You won't get him will you? I bet you don't even know where he lives.'

'It don't matter,' he says, hesitating. 'I can find him.'

'I can take you to him, if you let me go.'

'Why should I?'

'He was the worst wasn't he? Seeing her like that whenever he fancied?'

The boy says nothing, but I can see he is thinking about it.

'Where is he?'

'I'll take you there, and then will you let me go?'

He says that he will, but he is not completely convincing. No matter, since I have no idea where to find Quill. He sits back, allowing me to scramble from under him.

'I'm quick with this, you know,' he says, gesturing with the knife as I brush myself down.

'Don't worry,' I reply. 'I know.'

He stares me straight in the eye.

'Who are you?' he asks again, puzzled.

Who am I?

It begins upon Blackfriars, I am sure of that. I stand there upon the bridge and look down upon the water. There is no-one to stop me as I climb upon the stonework, no-one to watch as I plunge into the river. It is a common enough tragedy, after all. What is one more body when the current flows so fast downstream?

Who am I?

Flora Thorne? Natalie Meadows? No, it does not begin there; that is only the recent past. Take one step back, then another, then another. In truth, I can no longer recount the years nor remember how many times it has been; I cannot even recall all the reasons.

Who am I?

The river washes me clean, and I invent myself once more. I am nothing more than a part created and recreated at whim. There is no meaning to it, none that I can find, unless it is a punishment, a form of damnation; there is no way to redeem yourself, although I have tried every method.

I will do what I can for Ellen, all the same.

CHAPTER FORTY-EIGHT

GREEN LANES TO LAMBETH

'LAMBETH?' HE SAYS incredulously as we walk, a note of anger in his voice.

'I know it is a long way, but you agreed.'

We are nearing the Angel turnpike, and he sticks close to me, pressing the handle of the knife into my ribs.

'You said it weren't far.'

He sounds so like a child. I suppose he still is, barely.

'You said you saw her sing?'

'Ma used to take me to Brick Lane from when I was little. She was beautiful. She gave me her picture.'

He seems to be in a dream, remembering past glories. The knife is still close enough, however, against my side.

'And you followed her home?'

'One time I saw her, and I followed her, just to see. I saw her there . . .'

He stops, his little face contorted in disgust.

'I was in the tree, and I saw her . . . lying there. I didn't understand what they were doing until I went and saw the pictures.'

'You broke in?'

He laughs. I suppose it should be obvious by now.

We continue walking through Clerkenwell, towards the river, retracing the route I took the night he killed her. He sticks to me like glue, enjoying prodding me to let me know who is in charge. I keep stringing him along, assuring him we will find Quill. We do not pass many people; no doubt the ones who do see us may even take us for brother and sister. He remains quite taciturn until we approach the river.

'Did you know her?'

'Yes.'

'Why did she do them pictures like she was a whore?'

I pause, since I can only think of one answer. 'I think she was well-paid for it. I think she owed money.'

'Money?' he says, as if the very idea of it is novel to him.

'Shall we cross at Blackfriars?'

'If you like,' he says.

We come to the slope of the bridge, the gloomy gothic of new buildings at Westminster in one direction, the dome of St. Paul's in the other. There is no fog now and the sky is quite clear. The bridge itself is quite deserted. The boy is still close to me, but perhaps more trusting of me and not so alert. He is quite surprised, I think, when I jump clear of him and climb onto the balustrade in my bedraggled skirts.

'What you doing?' he asks, confused.

'I'm sorry, I lied,' I say goading him. 'I don't know where Quill lives, and I wouldn't tell you if I did.'

'Come back,' he says angrily.

'No,' I say, taking the photograph Quill had left behind from my pocket, waving it before his eyes. 'Do you see this? It's another picture of her. You won't get rid of it. I reckon there's lots of them. Everyone knows what she was doing. Everyone.'

'No,' he says, irritated, grabbing for the photograph. 'Give it here.'

I dodge him easily enough, snatching it away. He is angry now, angry enough for my purposes.

'Come on now, little boy, can't you take it?'

He scowls and comes at me swiping with the knife. I think he succeeds in cutting my leg, but he is quite baffled when I crouch down and embrace him as he lunges forward. His eyes are wide like saucers as I lean backwards, launching myself in the air, letting his momentum carry us both clear over the edge.

I cannot help but smile as he clutches the emptiness, swinging about wildly. To be safe, I hold him for as long as I can, although I doubt he can swim, and we sink quickly beneath the silt water. The black tides sweep around us once more, rolling me like a pebble in the stream, and, I think, I glimpse his dead face before the river closes my eyes.

Epilogue

Thomas Cave swings the boat against the early morning tide as dawn rises on the East End smoke stacks. The morning steamer has already left for Gravesend, and it is safe enough to ply this stretch of the river, though he knows the dangers of his work well enough. The current is strong, and he grunts as he pulls on the oars, scanning the shore of Rotherhithe and Wapping until he comes towards the high walls of the great docks, each of these fortresses abutted by dense forests of masts and rigging that gradually reveal themselves as ships, each with its own chaotic crowd of lightermen and stevedores, each of them ferrying an unending procession of crates and containers between boat and shore.

He stops in mid-stream, and it is then he sees her, swept up on the shore by the warehouses, pale and still enough to be a statue, washed up from the antique depths of the Thames.

He turns the boat towards the shore once more.

ALSO AVAILABLE IN ARROW

A Metropolitan Murder

Lee Jackson

The last train of the night pulls into the gas-lit platform of Baker Street underground station. A young woman is found strangled, her body abandoned in a second-class carriage.

The brutal 'Railway Murder' brings Inspector Decimus Webb to the newly-formed Metropolitan Line one bleak winter's night. His investigation leads him through the slums of Victorian London to the Holborn Refuge, a home for 'fallen women', and to Clara White, a respectable servant. As her past is revealed, Inspector Webb must decide whether she is merely a victim of circumstances, or prime suspect. Only then can he unearth a dark secret, hidden in the depths of underground London.

Lee Jackson's second novel brilliantly recreates the sights, sounds and smells of Victorian London, taking readers on a suspense-filled journey through its criminal underworld.

'Lee Jackson demonstrates quite brilliantly what the genre can do. This is a rare and succulent piece of work'
Literary Review

arrow books

ALSO AVAILABLE IN ARROW

The Welfare of the Dead

Lee Jackson

In the disreputable dance-halls and 'houses of accommodation' of 1870s London, a boastful killer selects his prey. His crimes seem like random acts of malevolence, but Inspector Decimus Webb, promoted to the Detective Branch at Scotland Yard, is not convinced.

Webb begins to suspect a connection between the terrible murders, a mysterious theft at the Abney Park Cemetery, and a long-forgotten suicide. His investigations lead him to the Holborn General Mourning Warehouse and its proprietor, one Jasper Woodrow, a seemingly respectable businessman.

As Webb delves into Woodrow's life, he uncovers layer upon layer of deceit. But can he unearth Jasper Woodrow's darkest secret in time to prevent another tragedy?

'A compelling and evocative novel that brings the past, and its dead, to life again'
Guardian

arrow books

arrow books